"Your lover told me all about you."

Karl's eyes narrowed. "Just another literary groupie looking for a big name to latch onto. After all, books are your world, aren't they, Beth? What would suit you better than a nice juicy writer to get your teeth into—even better than a nice juicy book?"

"And you believe what Nick told you," Beth said quietly.

"I don't know. I thought I was just Karl Franklyn to you, an unknown minor scribbler, and any attachment you had to me was purely personal. Nick insists you've known all along who I really am. He told me to ask you myself." He was fierce, accusing. "So I'm asking you. Do you know who I am, Beth?"

Rowan Kirby, mother of two teenagers, is happily married to an ex-research scientist, who takes care of the housework at their home near Bristol so that Rowan can concentrate more fully on her writing. She was born in Hong Kong but has spent most of her life living and working in London. She has a degree in English, and in the past has taught English as a second language to foreign students and been involved in adult literacy courses. But she's always had a passion to write. Her aim, she says, is to inject realism into the genre without losing sight of the romance.

Books by Rowan Kirby

HARLEQUIN ROMANCE
2675—SILENT STREAM
2758—HUNGER

These books may be available at your local bookseller.

Don't miss any of our special offers. Write to us at the following address for information on our newest releases.

Harlequin Reader Service
901 Fuhrmann Blvd.
P.O. Box 1325, Buffalo, NY 14269
Canadian address: P.O. Box 2800, Postal Station A,
5170 Yonge St., Willowdale, Ont. M2N 6J3

Hunger

Rowan Kirby

Harlequin Books

TORONTO • NEW YORK • LONDON
AMSTERDAM • PARIS • SYDNEY • HAMBURG
STOCKHOLM • ATHENS • TOKYO • MILAN

Original hardcover edition published in 1985
by Mills & Boon Limited

ISBN 0-373-02758-3

Harlequin Romance first edition April 1986

For Kathlyn and Victor Edwards (a Kent connection)

———————◆—◆———————

Printed in U.S.A.

CHAPTER ONE

BETH loved books. All kinds of books—fiction or fact, hardback or paperback, sophisticated or simple. They were her constant companions, her friends as well as her livelihood: an ideal combination.

And all the more ideal for Beth because they were so safe. She knew where she was with a book. Real life was full of bumps and pitfalls; real people let her down—but with a book she could feel secure. If she didn't like what it made her feel or think, she could just shut it away behind its covers and banish it back to its shelf. Out of sight, out of mind.

She seemed to have nursed this passion for the printed word all her life. As long as she could remember she'd been determined to work among literature—as a librarian, perhaps, or in publishing. When she left college in London, with a degree in English and no idea of what to do with it, she saw only one possible job advertised: assistant in a small bookshop in a northern suburb of the city.

On the face of it she could have done a lot better. The old man who owned the shop was too ill to put in more than an odd brief appearance; the place was tatty and held together by willpower and good faith; the pay was appalling. But harsh practicalities—such as future prospects, or financial status—came low on Beth's list of priorities. She always had been one of the world's dreamers.

When it came to selling books, however, she turned out to be a natural. Under her loving touch, the shop took on a clean new brightness. Customers drifted in to browse or to find a specific volume, and Beth never hassled or disturbed them, respecting their silent communication with the contents of her well-stocked shelves.

7

But they found it difficult not to be aware of the calm presence of this sweet-faced young woman who supervised them unobtrusively from her corner desk. If anyone asked her a question she'd look straight at them—shy but direct—out of those intelligent, enquiring dark eyes, taking her glasses off her small nose and chewing one earpiece thoughtfully as she considered. Then she'd offer a helpful, concise reply in a low, quietly firm voice—often accompanying it with a sudden bright smile which lit up her naturally solemn expression as though a 150-watt bulb had been switched on just behind it.

As a result, people usually stayed far longer than they'd intended in this peaceful atmosphere, surrounded by such a feast of books. Although there was no pressure to buy, it was hardly surprising that many of them left the shop with a whole armful of titles they'd never even heard of when they went in, let alone expected to take home. There was no conscious commercialism in Beth's approach. It wasn't her shop, after all, and her wage stayed the same whether she sold dozens or thousands. Neither she nor her employer ever gave a thought to incentive schemes or bonuses. Her success grew simply out of her sincere love for the product she was selling, and a desire to share that love with others.

So when, after a year, old Mr Whittaker's ill health finally got the better of him and he offered to sell Beth the shop at a nominal price, no one could have been more taken aback than she was. To work there, with a regular salary but little responsibility, was one thing; to actually own the place—to take on mortgages and business pressures and accounts and all that hard-headed stuff—that was quite another. She hummed and dithered, discussed it with her family and friends, turned it over in her mind a hundred times while the old gentleman awaited her decision. Then she screwed up her courage and confronted her bank manager with the proposition. The sum named sounded ridiculously cheap to him, and he advised Beth to go ahead, with his backing.

There were no excuses left for prevarication. She accepted, and Mr Whittaker retired gratefully to live with his married daughter in Cheam. Beth was on her own.

She made a roaring success of it, of course. After all, she'd been running the place more or less single-handed for months, gradually taking over stockchecking and ordering as well as selling. Mr Whittaker had employed a local firm of accountants, and the shop's income, though low, was efficiently organised. Under Beth's dedicated guidance, profits soon accrued in leaps and bounds. Within a year she'd virtually paid off the small bank loan. Another year, and she was doing very well indeed.

The bank manager's eyes lit up at the sight of the figures, and he congratulated himself on his own perspicacity in encouraging little Miss Porter to take the project on. As an afterthought he graciously congratulated the young lady herself on her achievement so far.

'Plough the profits back into the business,' he advised expansively, adding on a paternal note, 'don't let a little success, a little wealth, go to your head. Remember, Rome wasn't built in a day,' he warned platitudinously.

Beth had no intention of allowing anything at all to go to her head; but she nodded gravely, veiling the touch of irony which habitually sparked behind her gentle brown eyes. 'Thank you, Mr Hobson,' she said. 'I'll remember.'

And plough the profits back was exactly what she did. After nearly two years as proud owner of The Bookstore, she sat back and looked at her life with some surprise. Everything had worked out almost too satisfactorily. She had her independence—a precious commodity; a thriving business which she loved; a comfortable, well-appointed flat; a reasonably lively social life; friendships which weren't too intrusive or demanding ... and if there was a tiny, niggling awareness of an empty space, a hollow, somewhere at the very centre of it all—well, she could always bury herself in a book and it would fade into the background, right at the edge of her mind.

Until, suddenly, she couldn't do that any more. Inevitably perhaps, someone gatecrashed her ordered existence—pushing aside all her defensive layers, stepping straight into that small empty space and occupying it totally. Someone who took over and filled up her mind, her heart and her body—all three of which were so ripe and yet so inexperienced that it was like falling off a log; taking candy from a baby.

Instantly, her careful structure crumbled around her. Professionally, she just about kept her head above water; but personally, she sank right under. When the explosion came, she fell completely to bits—and the bits flew and swirled and flurried about her until she hardly knew where she was.

When the dust settled at last, she found herself to be miraculously still in one piece—albeit a rather battered and frayed piece. But she was no longer the owner of a little bookshop on the fringes of one of the greatest cities in the world. She'd been transported—almost, it seemed, by magic—to a larger, more luxurious bookshop in the centre of a prosperous, picturesque village among the rolling green fields of Kent. The Garden of England, and the county where she had grown up. As most creatures do when in shock or under stress, Beth Porter had headed instinctively for home.

Now, three years on, her life had sorted itself out into something resembling its original shape—though quieter, of course, in its more rural setting—and once again business was booming. Falconden was no sleepy hamlet, but a busy place full of diverse, lively minds— most of whom were proud of their very own bookshop, and patronised it willingly and generously. Then there were the summer visitors; and the people from miles around, whose villages weren't so well-endowed and who dropped in regularly to browse and buy.

Beth had no complaints. She soothed and cossetted her stunned inner self with reading and more reading, until very gradually the scar began to heal over. She decorated and furnished the small flat above the shop, creating a cosy home. She sat at her corner desk, avoiding close contact with anyone but customers and her family, who lived not far away; letting the rest of the complex world go by.

She commissioned a local signwriter to paint a starkly dramatic picture of a small black hawk, its talons clinging to a branch. *Falcon Books*. The sign swung proudly over the glazed door, symbol of Beth's regeneration. Safe inside her shop, surrounded by her beloved printed wares, surely nothing more could touch her?

Today, winter had suddenly arrived. November was only a week old, but eddies of wind howled up and down the High Street, playing with piles of dead leaves, carrying squalls of rain which beat against her windows as if they were determined to penetrate her cocoon inside. On a day like this the shop was more enclosing and inviting than ever. Beth pulled her chunky-knit jacket more tightly round her neat frame, pushed back the heavy fall of mid-brown hair (she thought of it as plain mouse, but under the light it glowed with every rich colour from gold to chestnut) from her round face, and buried her nose deeper in her novel. Not many people would be out at the shops this afternoon. It had been a busy summer; she could afford to relax.

The shop bell broke into her concentration as a customer pushed open the door. Beth glanced up, switching on her automatic expression of friendly enquiry. She never stood up or bustled about; in her experience, most people were far happier if she left them to browse on her own. They soon came over to ask her if they had a problem. The main thing was to let them know she was there, in charge, waiting to assist them if necessary.

Her smile widened into one of recognition and greeting. It was that young girl again—the one who'd been coming into the shop regularly the last few days. She'd spent ages looking round, and bought a couple of paperback teenage novels and a copy of *Pride and Prejudice* (an intriguing combination, Beth had privately thought); but they'd only exchanged the sort of superficial comments which tend to accompany commercial transactions. Remarks about the weather, prices, that kind of thing. She was, Beth thought, a remarkably pretty girl. Strikingly so, with her long blonde curls and delicate heart-shaped face.

At the same time there was a quality about her which caused Beth to feel distinctly uneasy. For a start, she didn't look at all well. She was unnaturally pale, her cheeks waxy and her blue eyes dull, listless, shadowed. There was a drawn tightness to her well-made mouth; and she was so thin! Tall—taller than Beth—but quite painfully bony under the thick sweater and tight jeans. There was nothing of her. A gust of that wind would surely blow her away.

But it wasn't only this sickly fragility which upset Beth. For some reason—and she couldn't, for the life of her, work out what it could be—she found herself gasping and flinching inwardly whenever this girl appeared. It wasn't like her, such an irrational reaction to a person, and she'd tried hard to trace the root of it; but so far she'd been unsuccessful. The girl herself was surely harmless and pleasant enough, but there was something about her which sparked off a memory . . . it was there, on the tip of her tongue, the brink of her consciousness, but it refused to surface. It was almost as if her mind had misted itself over, deliberately protecting itself from a painful association. Very strange, Beth mused. Very irritating, not to be in charge of one's own mind.

'Hi!' The girl was returning Beth's smile, but not with those wide blue eyes. Beth had already labelled her as American, probably about fifteen. Now she wondered, not for the first time, what a girl of this age was doing out of school in the middle of term.

Here it came again, that peculiar frisson, that unpleasant tingle to her nerves. She looked steadily at the girl, getting a grip on herself. After all, this was a customer, and it was no good giving way to crazy anxieties in front of one of those. 'Hallo,' she replied calmly. 'Sheltering from the storm?'

'It sure is blowing a gale out there,' the girl agreed. She shook the fair hair out of her troubled eyes and shoved her hands into her anorak pockets. 'You don't mind if I just look round, do you?' Uncertainty flickered across her normally deadpan expression, and Beth relaxed. She was hardly more than a child, this tall skinny creature. And no one who so obviously shared her own devotion to books could be all bad.

'Of course not. Help yourself. Feel free.' She smiled again, more warmly. The girl appeared to hesitate, and Beth found herself continuing. 'Live around here?' she prompted, slightly curious in spite of her natural reserve. Most Falconden faces were familiar to her by now; but until this girl's first visit a few days ago, Beth had never set eyes on her before. At least, she was pretty sure she never had.

'Yeah. At the moment.' The girl's face clouded. 'We may not be staying, but we're here for a few months. My father ...' She broke off and Beth raised an encouraging eyebrow. 'My father has some work to do, and he needs peace and quiet. My mother came from round these parts originally, so he ... we took a house on the edge of the village.'

That seemed to make sense. Beth's interest was captured, and she suspected it might be helping the girl, having someone to talk to. She closed the book she'd been reading and laid it on the desk. 'You're from the States, aren't you?' she suggested conversationally.

The girl was ready for that one. 'Canada,' she corrected promptly. 'It might be all the same to you,' she pointed out sternly, 'but to us it's very important.'

'Of course it is,' Beth acknowledged at once. 'Quite right too. I apologise—it must seem awful to you but we find it hard to tell the difference between the two accents. Now that I know, I'll listen out for it,' she promised.

'That's okay.' Again that oddly tragic little smile. 'No one here ever knows. I guess we Canadians get a bit touchy. Maybe it doesn't make all that difference.'

'Yes it does,' Beth contradicted firmly. 'The Welsh and Scots and Irish don't take kindly to being lumped in with the English. Canada's a vast country. Why should you put up with being labelled as American?'

The blue eyes regarded Beth with a new respect. 'That's a good point. The next person who says I'm making a fuss over nothing, I'll tell them that.'

'What part of Canada do you come from?' Beth was becoming more sociable than usual, following her hunch that the girl appreciated such everyday communication.

'Vancouver.'

Beth waited, but further information wasn't forthcoming. 'I've heard about British Columbia,' she observed. 'It sounds very beautiful.'

The girl shrugged, now avoiding Beth's eyes. 'I guess it's not so bad. I prefer it here, really.'

Beth hid her surprise. The girl might be a keen defender of her nationality, but she obviously had no nostalgia for her native land. She tried another tack. 'Don't you have to go to school while you're here?' she pressed cautiously.

'I was going to, when we came, but . . .' She shifted uncomfortably from one plimsolled foot to the other, still evading visual contact. 'I haven't been too well,' she mumbled. Then she seemed to rally, drawing herself up to her full, gangling height and facing Beth squarely. 'I've been ill,' she declared, as if defying Beth to deny it. 'I can't go to school.'

But Beth simply continued to study her thoughtfully, frowning slightly as she registered the conflicting emotions crossing the vulnerable young features. It was easy to feel warm pity for this girl. Unless Beth was much mistaken, she was as unhappy as she was unwell. 'I'm sorry to hear that,' she said sincerely. 'Are you on the mend now?'

'I dunno. I guess so.' Once again the blue gaze dropped and became masked. She really was disturbingly, hauntingly pretty. Hauntingly: that was the exact word. Beth found herself shuddering, as if a spectre had reached out a cold finger to touch her. A ghost from her own subconscious.

'What's your name?' the girl demanded unexpectedly, cutting into Beth's musings. She was curious, moody, unpredictable: just an ordinary adolescent.

This was clearly safer ground, and Beth was quite happy to follow her there. 'Beth Porter,' she supplied. 'Well, Elizabeth really, but I've always . . .'

'Beth!' Inexplicably, the girl's face had lit up. 'Say, that's a coincidence! You know what mine is?'

This was a tricky one. 'No idea. Not Beth as well?' That would have been too much.

'Oh no. Go on—guess. Have a guess.' She was quite excited. Some life had crept into the blue eyes, which even sparkled faintly in the gaunt face.

'I can't. Give me a clue.' Beth wasn't into guessing games, unless there was some point to them; and in this case she didn't know where to start trying.

'Well . . .' The girl thought for a moment, and then smiled triumphantly. 'One of my favourite books used to be called *Little Women*; and we're both in it.' She paused to let this sink in, and then added helpfully, 'Our surname is March.'

Beth grinned. 'Well, that certainly narrows the field down a bit. So, you've got to be Meg, Jo or Amy. Let me see . . .' She surveyed the girl, her head on one side. 'You don't look like a Meg or a Jo. I think you must be Amy.'

The girl giggled gleefully, transforming the thin, tense face. 'Right first time. Amy Franklyn.' She took a step nearer to the desk and held out a hand—very white, with long bony fingers. Beth reached over to shake it in her shorter, squarer ones. Amy's skin felt cold and clammy against hers. She certainly wasn't well, but this discovery had at least lent her a temporary animation. Basically, she must be a very lively girl. How sad, that she had to go through this ... ailment, suffering, whatever it was.

'I always wished I was Jo,' Beth confided. 'Beth was so feeble and pathetic. And she died in the end.'

'I wanted to be Jo, too,' Amy admitted, putting her hands back in her pockets as she relaxed. 'She was given all the best bits. She was much the most interesting. You could tell the writer liked her best. But Amy married Laurie, and I liked him better than the Professor.'

Beth accepted this somewhat unorthodox piece of literary criticism without argument. 'Don't you think the Professor was more romantic?' she suggested.

'Romantic?' The fair young brows arched sceptically; but Amy was too polite to divulge her real opinion of this middle-aged view of romance. 'Maybe,' she agreed doubtfully. 'But Laurie was young and handsome. He loved Jo,' she recalled wistfully, 'but Amy got him in the end.'

Beth was following her own train of thought. 'I must have read those books when I was about your age. Funny to think people are still reading them now, with so many new writers to choose from.'

'I read everything,' Amy announced firmly. At this moment a customer came in to choose a birthday card from the rack of tasteful ones which Beth kept at one corner of the shop; and while he was pondering, Amy proved the truth of her last remark by wandering up and down the shelves, stopping here and there to take out a book and flick through it.

As soon as the man had paid and left, she made a beeline back to the desk. 'How old are you, anyway?' she enquired, without embarrassment. Clearly her youthful confidence had been given a boost by this discovery of a mutual literary heritage.

Fortunately Beth wasn't the kind of woman to be put out by such an inquisition. 'Twenty-seven. How old are you?'

'Fourteen.' Amy was staring at her in undisguised amazement. 'Twenty-seven? But that's *old*! You don't look that old. You look about . . .' she considered, her blue gaze frank on Beth's face; 'twenty, maybe twenty-one. But twenty-seven! That's only eight years less than . . .' her voice dropped almost to a whisper, and she hung her head, tracing the pattern on the carpet with one foot. '. . . than my mother.'

Beth affected to ignore this sudden change of mood. 'Thanks a lot,' she said drily. 'I'm glad I don't look quite as decrepit as I am, at least.'

A faint blush swept up into Amy's pallid cheeks. 'Gee, I'm sorry, Beth—I never meant to . . . I mean . . . was that really rude?' She looked up, and then down again, and then around the room—everywhere but at Beth, who laughed aloud.

'Not at all. It's very nice to be told you look younger than you are.'

There was a slightly awkward pause while Amy allowed Beth's reassurance to encourage her own natural inquisitiveness. Then she resumed the interrogation. 'Is this your shop?'

'Yes.'

'All of it? All yours? No one else's?'

'That's right,' Beth acknowledged with quiet pride.

Amy was deeply impressed. 'All these books. That must be so wonderful.' She sighed, gazing round. 'And do you live here, as well? Do you have an apartment upstairs?' She looked up at the ceiling as if expecting it to be made of glass, revealing all.

'I have. And two rooms down here, behind the shop, too,' Beth informed her, enjoying the girl's appreciation.

'It must be great.' Amy frowned. 'But don't you ever get lonely, on your own?'

'No, of course not.' It sounded simple enough; but
even as she said it, Beth wondered if it was quite true. 'I
like it.'

Amy's attention was drawn away, her gaze travelling
over the shop. Now that the flush had faded from her
cheeks she seemed paler than ever. She swayed slightly,
and Beth half-rose to her feet, her own expression sharp
with concern. But Amy was turning away towards the
fiction shelves.

'Did you enjoy those teen romances?' Beth came out
from behind her desk and leaned against it, watching
Amy as she browsed.

'Yeah, I guess . . . but I'd sooner read something a bit
more serious. Like this, for instance.' She stopped and
picked out a heavy, hardback novel. 'Have you read
any of his?' She held it up for Beth to see.

Beth read the title: *The Iron Fist*, by Frank Charles.
Her reaction was instant and enthusiastic. 'Oh yes—
nearly all. I think he's marvellous. One of the few best-
selling authors today who can really write, but keeps a
good story going as well. And he seems so sensitive
about human nature. He understands things, and
makes you understand them. I love the way he delves
into what makes people tick. His books are unique, too.
Impossible to categorise. Have you read *Doublethink*?—
that's one of his best. A bit of science fiction, a bit of
romance, politics, adventure . . .'

She broke off, all at once acutely aware that Amy's
face had split into a grin. Was she laughing at Beth's
spontaneous outburst of praise—once again amusing
herself at the antics of the older generation? Beth bit her
lip and turned her head away. It wasn't like her to open
out so far or so readily—to a mere child, too, and one
she hardly knew; but Amy's simple question had caught
her on the hop. The author she'd picked out was one
Beth had always particularly admired—and when Beth
admired an author, it came close to something like
hero-worship. Where most people's private fantasy
worlds might include actors, film stars, pop singers,

Beth's had always been populated largely by brilliant writers. And Frank Charles happened to be one of them.

Still, that was no reason for going over the top. She levelled her tone out again, getting back in charge of herself and the conversation. 'Do you like him?'

For a moment there was silence, and Beth glanced over at Amy. The girl stood motionless, still clutching the book as if for support—her knuckles white where she gripped it with both hands. Her lips—bloodless, parted—seemed to grope for sound. Eventually she managed a murmur—one word, scarcely audible, 'Sure . . .' Then she slithered slowly to the carpet, as if all her hinged joints had collapsed at once, to lie in an inert heap between the rows of bookshelves. *The Iron Fist* fell from her nerveless fingers and lay open on the floor.

After a horrified, paralysed second, which seemed to stretch to minutes, Beth galvanised herself into action, leaping over to Amy, crouching beside her. What was it one had to do, for God's sake, when someone fainted? Lift her head, loosen her clothing, fetch water or brandy (not that she had any brandy), try the kiss of life, rub her hands to restore circulation? Struggling to keep calm, she pushed aside the damp anorak and the sweater, bending down to listen for a heartbeat. At first she could hear nothing, and she pressed closer, fighting back a wave of sick panic. Then the pulse came through to her, strong and clear. Whatever was wrong with her, Amy was very much alive. She had simply passed clean out.

Her own heartrate slowing down, Beth knelt up and took the girl's head between her hands, cradling it carefully in her lap, stroking and massaging the cold sticky cheeks and forehead with her warm fingers, willing life into her. At once Amy's eyelids moved, her eyelashes fluttered and lifted; she groaned and stared up into Beth's anxious face. 'What happened?' Her voice was thick and hoarse, her blonde hair matted at the temples with sweat.

'Hush,' Beth ordered gently. 'You fainted, that's all. Don't try to talk or move. You'll be all right in a minute.'

Apparently accepting the situation, and Beth's command of it, Amy lay still, her eyes closed, her breathing shallow but regular. 'I'm sorry,' she murmured.

There was something deeply touching about that small white face—so pinched, and yet so trusting. It seemed to have been part of Beth's life for so long—far longer than a few days—and still there was this sense of unease attached to it ... 'Don't be silly, Amy,' she admonished—but very kindly. 'You couldn't help it.'

'I guess not.' The words were like a little sigh, expelling itself in a puff of despair.

They stayed like that for another minute or two—strangely peaceful, utterly still. Beth watched intently as some faint colour returned to Amy's washed-out cheeks. Outside, the sky began to darken, and a restless wind still hurled handfuls of raindrops against window panes. She'd soon have to put the lights on. The greengrocer next door already had: she could see their comforting glow streaming across the wet pavement. Feet tapped and trudged and stomped past, scurrying to reach the dry warmth of home. For once Beth was glad it had been a slack afternoon; the way it had turned out, the last thing she'd needed was a shop full of customers.

As if in mockery of this train of thought, the shop bell clanged stridently as the door was flung open with quite unnecessary force. Damn, Beth thought; what a moment to choose to make an entrance! She jerked her head up, ready with warnings and explanations; but the words froze on her lips.

She knew at once, beyond doubt, that she'd seen him before. At the same time, she knew he was a total stranger. This time the note of jarring familiarity, the acute sensation of *déjà vu*, was far less unpleasant and alarming than the responses triggered off in her by poor

little Amy—but nonetheless, it was happening again.
Was she going mad? Had she entered some kind of
time-warp where each new person she met was doomed
to stir up these extraordinary half-memories of other
obscure, shadowy faces? The whole thing was bewilder-
ing, not to say ludicrous.

Not that there was anything superficially similar
about the man now dominating her shop, all but filling
up its doorway, and the girl lying next to her on the
floor. Rather, they were opposites: the negative and the
positive, the developed film and the print. Her hair
shone in fair, soft waves; his springing, coarse, near-
black mane tangled vigorously over the upturned colour
of his padded waterproof coat. Her skin was smooth,
translucent; his tanned, mapped with lines of suffering
and experience. Her eyes were innocent, limpid blue; his
hard, probing, rock-grey—encompassing the scene now
from a dark, sombre face. Her features were regular
and dainty; his sharply defined and deeply etched, from
high-bridged Roman nose to long carved lips. Amy was
tall for her age and sex, but painfully slight; this man's
height carried a matching breadth of shoulder, power of
muscle. Almost unconsciously Beth registered long legs
in lean drill jeans; driving gloves; jangling car-keys; and
the irrelevant fact that he wore insubstantial canvas
shoes, as if he'd rushed out into the rain in a tearing
hurry.

But her eyes were magnetised back to those
features—that strong, striking countenance, full of a
kind of detached arrogance which mingled incongru-
ously with something sensual, sensitive . . . it was so
memorable: where *had* she seen it before?

He hesitated briefly on the threshold, and gusts of
wind licked past him into the warm room. It was only a
slight second, but time enough for Beth to lay Amy's
head gently on the floor and scramble to her feet. The
instinctive urge to confront this intruder on his own
level—or as near to it as she could reach—was powerful
and overwhelming. Even when she stood, her eyes just

rested on the open neck of his shirt, the exposed skin at his throat.

His appearance might have been untimely and daunting; but Beth had never lacked spirit, and she leaped to defend her property, and Amy, and—for reasons she hardly began to understand—herself. 'Please close that door,' she ordered succinctly. 'Can't you see this young lady isn't well? We can do without a force nine gale in here, if you don't mind.'

For an instant that seemed an infinity, the granite gaze locked with her own alert brown one. Then it moved down to inspect her short, straight nose, and the large spectacle frames which insisted on slipping down to perch on the end of it; her compact chin, now defiantly lifted; the curtain of glossy hair which tumbled about her lively face and on to her slim shoulders. She felt it like a physical touch as it lingered on the full generosity of her mouth, then dropped to include the soft curves of her body beneath its simple skirt and jumper.

When he finally spoke, there was a clear irony underlining the wealth of concern in the deep rich tones. 'This young lady,' he echoed cynically, closing the door behind him and striding across to Amy, almost brushing Beth aside in his haste to reach the girl, 'happens to be extremely well-known to me; and so does her condition.'

His accent was quite unmistakably transatlantic. Before Beth's growing suspicions could harden any further, Amy was confirming them—stretching out her arms to him from the floor. 'Dad.' There was affection and pleasure in the weak greeting.

'Okay, honey, okay.' He knelt down, peeling off the gloves, thrusting the keys into his pocket. Then he gathered her up in his arms in a sweeping gesture, at once infinitely strong and infinitely tender. Beth stood to one side, rendered helpless, as she witnessed it, by a reaction which seemed to invade her whole self. She was so mesmerised, she couldn't even look away.

Swinging round, he was facing her again—standing tall, legs apart, holding his daughter tight against his chest. 'I'm sorry you've been troubled, Miss ...' he began, his tone starkly formal.

'Her name's Beth,' Amy interrupted drowsily, snuggling up to him. 'She's real nice, Dad.' She smiled wanly in Beth's direction. 'This is my father,' she explained unnecessarily. 'I'm sorry I passed out on you. I do it sometimes, but I didn't know I was going to do it today, or I wouldn't have ... I'd have stayed home.' She glanced up at her father, and then looked away, her mouth tightening. 'It's real stupid of me,' she muttered miserably.

'That's all right, Amy.' Beth cleared her throat, tingling under the scrutiny of those disconcerting, penetrating eyes. 'I'm glad you're better now.'

Amy's father set his precious burden down beside him with extreme care, supporting her firmly around the waist with his left arm so that she leaned her full weight against him as he offered his right hand to Beth. 'Karl Franklyn,' he introduced himself bluntly. 'Thanks for your help.' No smile reached his lips or his eyes, but the steely expression softened a little.

'Beth Porter.' His palm on hers was warm and dry; his grip on her fingers firm and hard. 'And I haven't done anything.'

'Just been here,' he pointed out tersely. 'She's told me about this place ...' He glanced round it appraisingly. 'She enjoys coming here. Guessed she'd be here now, but I didn't like the look of the weather, so I brought the car round. Hope you don't object to her visiting you?' he added, as if the thought had just struck him.

She pulled her hand away from where it still lay within his. 'Not in the least. Why on earth should I? Bookshops aren't a lot of use if no one visits them.'

He inclined his head slightly in acknowledgement of her statement—though she wasn't sure which part of it—but he made no reply. To her own surprise she heard herself continuing, her eyes on Amy, 'I'm sorry she's ill, Mr Franklyn. If there's anything I can do . . .'

Blushing, she turned away. It was quite unlike her to involve herself in other people's problems voluntarily—and after all, these were strangers to her. But there was something compulsive, charismatic about this forceful man and his frail pretty daughter. Against her better judgment, she caught a corner of her mind wondering what the girl's mother, waiting at home, might be like. Like Amy, surely: blonde and beautiful, tall and slender—a fitting match for Karl Franklyn.

'That's good of you, Miss Porter. We manage quite well; but we'll certainly remember your offer.' Was there a hint of wry satire beneath that tough, gruff tone? Beth was usually quick at getting the measure of people, but this man was impossible to work out.

He became brisk again. 'Now, young woman. Better get you home. Can't have you wandering all over the village, collapsing in shops, inconveniencing the good folk of Falconden.' He picked her up again, with no trace of effort, carried her over to the door and opened it with the fingers of one hand, shifting Amy up in his grasp in order to do so but keeping his hold no less tight. 'Goodbye, Miss Porter. Apologies again for the disruption.' He threw the words at her over his shoulder as he propped the door open with one elbow in order to edge Amy carefully through the gap.

' 'Bye, Beth!' Amy's voice just reached Beth over the clang of the shop-bell as the door closed behind them. Before Beth could muster any words at all, let alone say them, Karl and Amy Franklyn had disappeared along the rain-swept street.

CHAPTER TWO

FOR a full minute Beth stood staring after them. Then she shrugged, walked to the door, locked and bolted it and turned the notice round to 'closed'. It was six o'clock, and she usually reckoned to shut up shop around five-thirty. Today might not exactly have been throbbing, business-wise; but it had certainly had its dramatic moments otherwise. Enough food for thought there to last all night, probably several nights.

And talking of food, it was time she fixed herself something. Her stomach was rumbling, complaining that all she'd put into it since breakfast was several cups of coffee, a thin crispbread or two and some cottage cheese. Hardly enough, it pointed out tetchily, to enable it to do its job of holding body and soul together. Beth enjoyed her food and had a healthy appetite; but living alone, it wasn't always easy to be bothered to cook properly. It would have been only too simple to hop into her little Fiat and drive over to her parents' farm, not many miles away. She knew her mother would always be glad to stretch the family supper to include her oldest daughter. But Beth had her pride, and a strong sense of independence and self-discipline, and she made a point of preparing herself a decent meal most evenings.

She turned back now to gaze into the empty shop. It felt emptier, more silent than ever after the events of the past hour. She tidied her desk, locked up the till and crossed towards the back of the shop. On the way, she nearly tripped over the book which still lay open on the floor where Amy had dropped it as she fell. Beth stooped to pick it up, lovingly smoothing out the dust-jacket before replacing it in its slot on the shelf.

As she held it in her hands, her attention was arrested

by the photograph of the author, brooding out at her from the back flap. As a fan of his work, she'd studied it before: darkly handsome, cynically lowering. And suddenly joltingly familiar. She gasped: this was him! This was the same face that had left her own shop, not ten minutes ago!

Colour drained from her cheeks and then almost at once flooded back again in a pink tidal wave. Pieces of a puzzle were falling miraculously into place; she cursed herself for several kinds of a fool not to have spotted them earlier. That instant sense of recognition as soon as he'd appeared—and yet the powerful impact of his presence in the flesh, quite obviously new to her ... Amy's acute interest in his books, unusual in a teenage reader, and her pleased grin when Beth indulged in such extravagant approval of his writing ... even his name, which might have given her clue: Frank Charles—Karl Franklyn. It stood out a mile, once you'd realised. He must have been having a quiet laugh at her expense, somewhere behind that grim façade—that natural concern for his daughter. Beth winced with embarrassment to contemplate it.

On second thoughts, maybe it wasn't quite as stupid as all that, not to have guessed. There hadn't been so many hints, after all, not if one wasn't on the lookout for them—and she certainly hadn't been. No, surely he'd never expect her to penetrate his disguise, just by recognising his face—not with all the thousands of books and authors inhabiting her shop.

Relaxing, she allowed a slight smile of excitement to creep across her face. Here he was, a man whose creative genius she'd admired for years, living in her own village; perhaps crafting the next piece of work right on her doorstep! And today he'd actually set foot in her shop, and she'd become friendly with his child. It was difficult not to feel conspiratorial. How many other local people would know who he was? Not many, she was prepared to swear. He didn't look the kind who'd willingly divulge his identity to all and sundry. He'd keep his privacy tightly guarded, and he'd expect his wife and family to do the same. If Amy had been about to give the game away, it was just as well for her that she'd fainted when she did. At least no one could now accuse her of tactlessly letting the truth out to Beth.

It was a pity he'd turned out to be such an overbearing, unbending man—but perhaps, with a brilliant mind like that, you had to make some allowances. In any case, his secret was safe with Beth. Her discovery wouldn't make any difference to the fact that she'd like to help Amy if she could, whatever was wrong with the poor girl. With any luck, it wouldn't be necessary to confront the father too often in the process of befriending the daughter. Obviously he'd regarded today as a kind of emergency, what with the weather, and Amy feeling so ill, and Beth and her shop being unknown quantities.

She sighed as she slipped *The Iron Fist* back into its place on the shelf, suddenly very tired. So, that was one of today's mysteries sorted out; but it still left another, even stranger one—her painful, elusive response to Amy herself. It seemed to happen at a deeper level altogether, but Beth was determined to get to the bottom of it. She'd push it to the back of her mind for now—try to stop worrying at it—and most probably the solution would hit her out of the blue; and it would be something equally simple.

That night she tossed restlessly as the dark, potent face and form of Karl Franklyn, alias Frank Charles, haunted her dreams; fading in and out of the picture, alternating with the sad pale countenance of his daughter—the two images superimposing on to each other like ghosts in a corny thriller movie. And somewhere among or between them was the suggestion of a third image—so near, and yet so far from Beth's recognition. She awoke sweating and shaking, fighting her way up through layers of unconscious to try and make some sense of her brain's garbled messages. She knew she was getting there; but so far they still escaped her.

Saturday was always her busiest day, with the children out of school, and she spent a hectic morning attending to a shopful of eager young customers. She had a whole corner devoted to children's books, and she liked to encourage them to read by allowing them to sit and browse and find out what they liked—adding to the attractive atmosphere with colourful posters and changing exhibitions.

The weather brought a boost to business by improving dramatically overnight into a clear, cool autumnal crispness. Beth knew she should never complain when trade was brisk, but this morning it took more strength of character than usual to treat everyone with the friendly efficiency they'd come to expect.

At one o'clock, with some relief, she locked the door and turned the sign round. She couldn't afford to lose a Saturday afternoon's takings—a fact which limited her weekend activities, not that she really minded that; but at least she could take a nice long lunch break, enjoying a leisurely snack and putting her feet up until two-thirty. One day soon, she meditated as she made her way back across the deserted shop, she'd have to see about finding a part-time assistant: a bright local girl to help out at busy times, eventually even give Beth the odd weekend off.

Her musings were interrupted by the sound of tapping on the window. Swinging round, she saw the sun gleaming on bright curls—a youthful, skinny, bejeaned figure—an anxious little face peering through the glass. Amy had come looking for her again; and Beth smiled with genuine pleasure at the sight.

She waved and walked back to the door, unlocked it and stood aside to let her visitor in. 'Glad to see you're on your feet again. You nearly missed me.' Her greeting was warm but matter-of-fact, suggesting that the girl would be welcome any time. 'I've just closed for lunch.'

Slightly breathless, Amy watched as Beth locked up again. 'I never thought . . . I just thought you'd be here. Do you always take a lunch hour?'

'Oh yes,' Beth confirmed emphatically. 'I need a rest, and I wouldn't want to go without a bite to eat. Very important, even if I don't have much. But if you ever arrive too late to catch me, you can always come round to the side door and ring the bell.' She led the way through to the back of the shop and up the narrow staircase to her kitchen.

'Is that your own door, to your private apartment?' Amy's trainers padded softly up the carpeted stairs behind Beth.

'That's right. Just ring, and if I'm in I'll come down. Any time.'

'Gee, thanks Beth. I'd like that.' Amy sounded almost overwhelmed by such easy hospitality. For the child of such a famous father, she seemed singularly unspoilt. Beth smiled privately to herself: it still tickled her, the idea of sharing a secret with Frank Charles— but she wasn't telling Amy that she knew. Her relationship with the girl must be at a strictly personal level—especially as Amy was well aware of Beth's high opinion of the man's writing.

And anyway, the man doubtless spent most of his time sitting behind a typewriter behind closed doors. If anyone had brought the child up well, it was more likely to be her mother. Beth wondered, in passing, why a momentary consideration of Mrs Karl Franklyn should cause her a brief but unpleasant tingle.

In the tidy, airy kitchen, Amy watched in silence as Beth took out a loaf, butter, milk, a box of eggs and a mixing bowl. The girl's expression was curiously shuttered—wary even, Beth noted; her cheeks paler than ever. 'I was just going to scramble myself some eggs,' Beth explained blandly. 'I hope you'll join me?' She broke two of the eggs neatly into the bowl, picked up a third and glanced at Amy as she awaited her reply.

Amy was staring down at her hands—long thin

fingers twisted tightly together on the wooden table top. She shook her head slightly, but made no attempt to speak.

Surprised, but keeping her tone absolutely steady, Beth went on, 'Of course I could make an omelette if you like that better. Or any kind of egg—boiled, poached, fried?' Still Amy's lips were pressed together, and she refused to look up and meet Beth's eye. 'Just a piece of toast?' Beth suggested, putting the egg down and pouring a little milk into the bowl. 'Cheese? Are you one of the many people who don't like eggs in any form?'

Amy shook her head, and muttered—so softly that Beth had to strain forwards to pick the words up—'I'm not very hungry.'

'I should have thought of that—you ate before you left home, I expect.' Beth added salt and pepper and began to attack her mixture energetically with a whisk. 'Well, in a minute we can put the kettle on and have a cup of coffee—or tea, whatever you like,' she invited cheerfully. 'As long as you don't mind watching while I eat mine.'

At last Amy's face lifted and her blue gaze allowed itself to rest on Beth's warm brown one. Her expression of sheer relief was startling, out of all proportion—as if a serious crisis or threat had been narrowly averted. 'Thanks,' she murmured; then she watched with a kind of fascination as Beth put bread in the toaster, warmed some butter in a small pan and began to cook the eggs carefully.

'Do you like cooking?' Beth spooned the creamy yellow-gold concoction on to two slices of toast. 'Or do you find it as boring as I did at your age?' Amy still seemed to be having difficulty getting words together, so Beth laughed and went on. 'I was happy enough to eat the stuff, as long as someone else did all the work.' She glanced at Amy, and paused with a forkful halfway to her mouth. Then she continued to eat, wisely deciding it was better not to probe the girl's very real discomfort. No doubt she'd open further in her own good time, when Beth had won her trust.

Amy cleared her throat as Beth finished up the last piece of toast, conscious that the blue eyes had been riveted on every mouthful she chewed. 'I don't . . .' she croaked huskily. 'I don't eat much.' Beth's eyes were drawn to the fragile, bony frame opposite her. That much was patently obvious, she reflected; but she said nothing, leaving Amy to communicate at her own pace. 'I don't . . . I don't like to eat, really.' There was pain and anxiety in her face as she made this simple claim.

Beth pushed her plate aside and leaned her elbows on the table, chin in hands, regarding Amy solemnly from over her glasses—which had, as usual, slipped down to the end of her nose. 'You'll fade away, Amy.' The remark was only half in jest. A shadow of concern tightened the soft mouth, hardened the gentle gaze. 'Even if you're not well, your body's got to have fuel or it can't build itself up, or even function—and neither can your brain. And especially when you're still growing. But you must know that, surely? I expect your parents tell you the same.'

Amy shook her head again, and there was a stubborn set to her expression. 'Sure—people tell me, all the time. But they can't make me do what I don't wanna do. No one can make me eat, or do anything, if I don't choose to.' Her tone rose to a sudden crescendo of hostile panic. 'And neither can you!' she cried violently.

Warning lights had begun to flash inside Beth's head as an early suspicion took shape in her mind. She had more than a vague notion what this girl might be suffering from. 'Her condition . . .' her father had said: and that was just what it was. A condition, a well-known, universally-feared syndrome, most common in adolescent females. Anorexia Nervosa. Fear of eating. A pathological refusal to force food down; a grim deep-rooted determination to stay thin and slight at all costs. An alarming Greek and Latin name for a terrifying mental and physical state.

No wonder Amy was frail and white and went around collapsing, if she was constantly undernourished—perhaps hardly nourished at all. No wonder her father found it necessary to rush out after her, keeping tabs on her, making sure she was all right. Beth's tender feelings went out to the girl—and also to her parents. What a dreadful worry it must be, to have to see one's child going through such a torment! And how they must suffer, too, since her refusal to eat the food they offered and prepared must surely seem like a personal rejection of their loving care?

Unless, of course, their loving care wasn't generous enough? Searching her memory for information she'd gleaned on the subject from her wide reading, Beth recalled that the condition arose from emotional problems as often as not. Like so many apparently physical ailments, it usually sprang direct from more complex psychological areas. But Karl Franklyn certainly didn't give an impression of an uncaring father. Far from it; he had struck Beth as fiercely protective and devoted—and Amy had seemed to return his affection with no apparent resentment.

Well, it wasn't for Beth to leap to conclusions or pass judgments. If she wanted to involve herself in the girl, she must win her confidence gradually—reassure her that she presented no threat or pressure. After all, there might be more to Amy's illness than this. She must wait until Amy was ready to tell her.

Now she simply stood up, carried her empty plate to the sink and rinsed it. Then she filled the electric kettle and switched it on. 'Of course not—and I'm sure no one wants to,' was all she said, in answer to Amy's outburst. 'Now, how about a cup of coffee? I expect you do have to drink, from time to time,' she observed sardonically.

Amy had subsided, pathetically crumpled and defeated in the face of Beth's unruffled acceptance of her declaration. 'I'll have a cup of tea, please,' she conceded grumpily, as if giving way in a major battle.

'If that's okay,' she added, remembering her manners—as well as the fact that she liked Beth a lot, and that sympathetic friends were hard to come by.

'Of course it's okay. I'm very fond of tea myself. Nothing like it, actually.' Beth chattered on as she warmed the teapot and spooned tealeaves into it, reaching up into a cupboard for a barrel-shaped tin. 'I've got some digestives in here, I think. My favourites. It's all right,' she went on, catching Amy's paranoid glare, 'I won't even offer you one—don't worry!'

She poured the tea and sat down again opposite Amy, pushing the sugar bowl over to her in a nonchalant gesture, opening the tin and helping herself to a biscuit. Out of the corner of her eye she noted that Amy was loading her cup furtively with two heaped spoonsful of sugar, and she struggled to hide her pleased reaction. Good; at least that was a small boost to her instant energy supplies, even if not of any basic nutritional value.

Acting on impulse—she very rarely had more than one—Beth took another biscuit from the tin and crunched it noisily. 'Sometimes,' she admitted with a grin, 'I like to dunk these in tea or coffee. But I realise it's not done in the best circles, so I'll wait till I get to know you better.'

'Oh, I don't care about things like that,' Amy assured her airily, as Beth had hoped she might; and to her private delight, the girl reached over, grabbed a biscuit from the tin, dunked it defiantly in her teamug until it was soft—and ate it; quickly, with more evidence of obstinacy than enjoyment—but at least she ate it.

It took every ounce of Beth's willpower not to comment. But she knew it was vital to play the whole thing right down, so she merely grinned at Amy again and sipped her tea. In the next five minutes Amy consumed six more biscuits, dunking each one and then wolfing it down as fast as possible; her face deadpan and pale, but her eyes—when Beth allowed herself a quick glance up—agitated, fearful, angry.

Neither of them said a word about it, but as Beth bustled about afterwards, clearing up the kitchen, she was uncomfortably aware of Amy's look of total, black fury. No doubt she was hating Beth for encouraging her to eat something; and perhaps loathing herself even more for her weakness in giving way to hunger pangs just for once.

A few biscuits wasn't exactly a feast, mind you; but at least the girl had refuelled a little—enough to prevent her passing out again; and Beth understood now just how often that must tend to happen.

'Well.' Beth sat down again, consulted her watch and smiled at Amy, ignoring her bad-tempered frown. 'There's still nearly an hour before I need to open up again. What would you like to do? Just talk? Or . . .' an idea struck her, 'would you like to come and look at some of the books I keep in store? I've got some rather special ones,' she explained enticingly, 'some old rare editions, and some expensive coffee-table glossies which I don't want people handling. I have the covers on display but they have to ask if they want to see the actual books.'

Amy's mood made a magical recovery from gloom to enthusiasm at this suggestion. 'Great. I'd like to see your store-room, Beth. I'd like to learn how you run the shop and everything.' She sighed wistfully. Beth recognised the symptoms of a clever child, star-struck on books, and she warmed to the girl more than ever. 'I wish I had a whole shop full of books.'

Beth laughed as she led the way from the kitchen. 'It's fine—but it's a big responsibility too. And lots of hard work, even if you're a confirmed bookworm. There's more to it than just sitting around all day reading, you know.'

'Oh sure. But if you've got to be selling something, it might as well be a thing you really love,' Amy pointed out, with the wisdom of youth.

Out of the mouths . . . there really wasn't anything wrong with this child's intelligence. Beth turned to smile at her. 'That's very true,' she agreed. In many ways, she reflected, Amy was more like a miniature adult than an adolescent.

Beth's stockroom was immediately behind the shop itself. 'Here you are!' She waved an expressive arm around her loaded shelves. 'Browse to your heart's content. I know there's no need to remind you to treat them carefully,' she added lightly.

Amy was staring, her blue eyes round with transparent joy. 'I'll treat them ... reverently,' she declared; and Beth knew she meant it. There was genuine understanding in the smile they exchanged. With common ground like this, Beth thought, how could she fail to help this girl? But how could she do it, without invading the privacy of a family to whom she was a complete outsider?

And then it seemed obvious, the plan which appeared in her mind, ready formulated—as if it had been there all along. A new interest, that was what Amy needed, to take her mind off her unhappy obsession with food—or rather, the absence of it. Without pausing to consider, Beth found herself saying, 'How would you like to help me out in the shop sometimes, Amy? I could do with a bit of assistance, especially late afternoons when school's out, and Saturdays. If you're not too busy ...?'

Amy's answer blazed out from her eyes. 'Oh Beth! I'd love it, I really would. Are you sure—I mean, I wouldn't just be in the way?' Her face clouded almost as fast as it had lit up. 'You're not just suggesting it to—make me happy?'

This was a little too close to the mark for comfort, but Beth shrugged it off with a flippant grin. 'For one so young and tender, Miss Franklyn, you have a suspicious nature. Keeping you happy never crossed my mind,' she lied blithely. 'I'm not a registered charity, for God's sake. I'm asking you because I could use the help, and because I like you and I think you'd do it well.' That, at least, was perfectly true.

'Sorry.' Suitably chastened, Amy turned away. 'It's just that . . . they keep trying to . . . I'm not . . .'

'It's okay, love.' Relenting, Beth laid a gentle hand on one skinny shoulder. 'I understand. Mind you,' she moved away to pick up a pile of books and move them to a tidier corner, 'I couldn't pay you—not officially, anyway. It's against the law—I'd be had up for exploiting an under-age person. Slave labour. It would have to be a private arrangement, between you and me. And your parents, of course,' she added quickly. 'We must check up that we don't . . .'

But Amy's fair brows had shot up in disgust. '*Pay* me?' she exploded. 'I don't want *money*! I'm not short of cash—I get an allowance. I don't need money, Beth. We've got plenty. That's not why I . . .' She moved her hands in agitation.

'Of course it isn't,' Beth soothed. This was a volatile creature, sure enough. Even more prickly and touchy than your average adolescent—and Beth knew enough about the breed to know how unpredictable they usually were. Perhaps she'd inherited the trait from one or other of her parents; or both.

On top of that, at moments of tension such as this, there was still that discordant note—this sharp, undefined familiarity—reaching out to Beth from the girl. She stifled a shudder, internalising it at once so that Amy wouldn't notice. 'I never meant to trample on your sensibilities, Amy. I just thought I should mention it now rather than later—I have to have things straight from the start.'

'Sorry,' Amy muttered for the second time in five minutes. 'Dad always says I should count to ten before I shoot my big mouth off. I guess he's right, as usual.'

Once again, she lifted her expression in an instant from despondency to pure, infectious charm. Once again, the sight stirred strange twinges in Beth's memory. 'Don't change your mind about the offer, will you, Beth—because of my temper? I'm not really like that,' she wheedled. 'I'll be all sweetness and light to the customers, I swear. I can be a real angel when I put my mind to it—you'd be amazed. Dad calls me his Pollyanna.' Beth could imagine that—and the cynical tone it would be spoken in. 'You won't know how you ever managed without me,' Amy was pulling out all the persuasive stops now; not that she needed to. It took more than a few heated words to make Beth change her mind.

Beth waited for the eager words to finish jostling each other, her dark eyes alight with amusement as they rested on the girl's hopeful face. 'Don't get so worked up, Amy,' she advised quietly. 'A few home truths never did anyone any harm. And my mind's not as easy to shift as that, once I've set it on something. But it does depend on what your parents say. Now,' she continued briskly, before Amy could pursue the subject, 'let me show you round a bit. This is where the really important things happen.' She indicated a wall stacked with brand-new, shining volumes. 'This is where I put all the titles which have recently come in, before I get round to displaying one of each in the shop. I had a delivery yesterday, and I haven't got any further than unpacking them yet. You could help me decide what to leave here, and what to move straight through, and where they should go, if you like.'

Amy's eyes glowed. 'I'd like that. Do you put all the books by the same author together? Or do you divide them into subjects, or what?'

They were soon happily engrossed in some of the technicalities involved in running a successful shop, and Amy was a quick pupil. It was going to be a pleasure, Beth decided, to have her around.

The strident note of an electric bell pealed through their concentration. Amy stared at Beth, her eyes wide and startled. 'What's that?'

'Only my doorbell—the one to my flat—damn!' Beth frowned. 'I'm not expecting anyone. People usually leave me alone in the lunch-hour, unless they 'phone first. Could be Sal or Lynne, I suppose. One of my sisters,' she explained, as Amy's expression became even more anxious. 'They do look in sometimes if they're in the village on a Saturday.'

'Your sisters?' Amy pouted enviously. 'I wish I had a sister. Or even a brother might be better than nothing.' She sighed deeply. Life was unfair.

Poor sad, singular kid, Beth thought. But she said cheerfully, 'So you're a lonely only? You ought to be grateful. Big families can be great, but they can be a real bind. I'm the oldest of five, so I should know.' The bell shrilled again, louder and longer, and she clicked her tongue in irritation. 'I'll have to go and answer the summons. They sound urgent, whoever they are. Don't worry, I won't let them keep me long. I must open the shop soon, anyway.' She turned as she reached the door. 'Want to come with me—or will you stay and carry on sorting out these books? You're doing a grand job.'

'I'll stay, thanks. If you trust me with all these first editions and things.' Amy grinned happily as she returned to her task, now thoroughly absorbed.

'See you in a minute then.' Beth ran down the corridor, round the corner and into the narrow entrance hall to open her private front door.

Her spontaneous smile of enquiry faded as she confronted her visitor. It wasn't either of her sisters. It wasn't even female. Dominating her threshold loomed the powerful form and forbidding expression of Amy's father.

'Mr Franklyn.' Beth recovered her composure at once, raising calm brown eyes to meet stony grey ones. 'What a surprise.' She stood aside politely to let him in, but he stayed where he stood, both hands thrust deep into the pockets of his coat.

'Is Amy here?' he demanded brusquely, without preamble.

Beth prickled at his offhand manner; but she maintained her steady gaze upon his face. 'As a matter of fact she is. I thought you must know, or I'd have got her to 'phone and tell you. She's quite all right,' she added, catching his frown of concern. 'She's not being any trouble, in fact . . .'

'In that case, perhaps I'd better come in, if you don't mind.' He looked and sounded as if that was the last thing on earth he wanted to do. Beth hardly knew whether to feel amused or offended.

The former was usually safer, so she settled on that. 'I don't mind in the least.' She stepped back and he strode past her, permitting himself the merest cursory glance round as he entered the hallway—immediately dwarfing it.

'Up here?' Without waiting for her reply, he'd already set off up the stairs—taking them two at a time—and was near the top of the first flight before he realised she wasn't following him. Then he turned and stared down at where she stood, patiently waiting on the lowest step. 'I saw the shop was shut, so I assumed you'd be in your apartment,' he pointed out gruffly.

Smiling slightly, Beth began climbing the stairs towards him. 'As it happens, we were downstairs in my stockroom,' she remarked mildly. 'But since you've got that far already, and I wouldn't mind a quick word with you, perhaps it isn't such a bad idea to come up—it'll have to be quick, though, or she'll . . .'

His frown deepened. 'Did you say you were in the stockroom?'

'That's right. Behind the shop.'

'With Amy?'

'I was showing her where new books go.' She caught up with him at the top of the staircase, leaning on the bannister as she confronted him.

'I thought you said she wasn't being any trouble?'

'And I meant it. She's a sweet girl, and she loves books, and she could be a real help to me in the shop . . .' She sensed him stiffen, and curbed her eager tongue. 'That's what I wanted to ask you about, if you can spare a minute.'

'Hmmm.' He made no further comment beyond a

sceptical grunt. Pushing past him in the small space at
the top of the stairs in order to lead him to her sitting-
room, Beth felt every sinew of her body tighten at the
inevitable contact. She told herself not to be such a
fool. Amy was a young girl who might experience
strange flutterings at the touch of a virile man; she, on
the other hand, was a mature woman who had lived
and loved and knew what life was all about—and ought
to know better.

'Sit down,' she invited coolly as they entered the
bright comfortable room. 'I won't keep you long. I
promised Amy I'd only be a few minutes, and I've got
to open the shop in about a quarter of an hour.'

He folded his length into her largest armchair and sat
forwards, tense, his long hands resting on his knees. She
perched opposite him on the edge of her gold velour
sofa.

'What's all this,' he barked, again wasting no time on
useless courtesies, 'about Amy helping in the shop?'

Again Beth bristled at his tone, but kept herself under
control, facing him firmly and calmly. 'Mr Franklyn,
I'm not suggesting she tires herself out, or works night
and day—just that she might spend a bit of time here. It
would give her an interest—something really useful to
do—and I know she'd enjoy it.'

'What makes you think she requires an interest?' He
was still gruff and brisk, but she didn't miss the deep
involvement which flickered in his eyes as he talked
about his beloved daughter.

It was like tiptoeing over hot nails, trying not to
trample on his overdeveloped sense of pride and
privacy. 'Well, she doesn't go to school—presumably
because of her illness,' she ventured, choosing each
word with care.

'Also because, as temporary residents in this country,
we are not obliged to send her,' he cut in edgily.

Beth wasn't at all sure about that; but she let it pass.
'She has a real feeling for literature, and she wouldn't
be in the way. I think she'd love it, and I think . . .'

'Yes?' he prompted as she hesitated—his eyes fiercer than ever, but hooded as he followed her every syllable.

'I think,' she continued more firmly, lifting her head to return his stare, 'it might help her.'

'You consider her to be in need of help?' He wasn't making this any easier. It was like trying to grab hold of a wet, slippery rock.

Beth drew in a deep breath. 'I don't know her well yet, of course—or all her circumstances, but . . .'

'No,' he agreed tersely. 'You don't.' Looking at him, she could almost see the bubble with *Mind your own business* printed in it issuing from his dark unruly head. Anyone would think she was asking him a favour, rather than offering one.

Goaded suddenly into anger at his attitude, she allowed her spirit to show itself. 'Mr Franklyn.' She emphasised each word heavily. 'I really do feel that helping me in the shop could turn out to be just what Amy needs. I know she's not strong . . .'

'She hasn't been at all well,' he interrupted rudely. 'We have to be careful.'

Beth sighed. She'd expected to be up against some opposition, but not this degree of obstruction. She leaned towards him, taking off her glasses as she intensified her gaze upon his face—her own concern for the girl lending extra animation, a delicate flush, to her expression. 'Why did you come looking for Amy again today?' She tried a new tack, taking a chance, following a hunch. 'It's a lovely day, not too cold, and it won't be dark for hours yet, and you knew she'd probably come here, after yesterday . . .'

It worked. 'She hasn't had any lunch.' His reply was razor-sharp, cutting straight to the point—and yet, as Beth well knew, evading the true issue. 'Also, she went out this morning without breakfast. I—she shouldn't be allowed to . . .'

'Actually,' Beth announced, 'she's had some lunch here. With me.' Regarding him steadily, she watched as veiled, hostile irony turned to open disbelief. 'Oh, not much—just some tea and a few biscuits. But better than nothing. She didn't fancy eggs, so . . .'

'She had something to eat? Here?' Sheer amazement penetrated his guard for a moment. 'Did she seem—er—hungry, then?'

'I was having lunch anyway, so naturally I offered her some,' Beth said simply. Then, when he seemed lost for words, she took the plunge and carried on. 'I know what's wrong with Amy, Mr Franklyn. You don't have to protect her from me. I'm on her side. It would be a waste of your time and mine. I like her a lot, and I think she trusts me, and I'd really like to help her, if I can.'

There was open, intense curiosity in his eyes now. 'So, what's wrong with her then, Miss Porter?'

It was a direct challenge, and she willingly took it up. 'She's anorexic, isn't she?'

For a moment he was silent. Then the long mouth hardened and twisted down at one corner, and he lifted both hands, palms upwards, in a wry gesture of resignation—acceptance, almost—before dropping them to his knees again. 'She didn't tell you herself, did she?' There was the barest hint of admiration, now, lacing the tough tone.

'Good Lord no. She doesn't even know I've guessed. But it's not very difficult when you know a bit about the condition.'

'And you do?' His interest in her genuinely aroused now, he leaned back in the chair, relaxing a little.

'Only from reading, keeping my ears and eyes open—not from first hand,' she hastened to explain. 'Poor kid, she must be going through a bad time.'

'It's not easy,' he acknowledged grimly, 'for any of us.'

She nodded her head in sympathy. 'No, it can't be. Anyway, now perhaps you'll understand why I thought a few hours spent here with me might be just what she needs to bring her out of herself. Naturally, I told her it would have to be discussed with you and your wife first—I'd have 'phoned you later, but since you turned up on the doorstep I thought there was no time like the present to . . .'

'Take the bull by the horns?' he suggested drily.

'Something like that. So, what do you think?' she pressed eagerly.

'Well,' he drawled, 'since you've displayed such kind concern for my daughter's welfare—and such perspicacity in diagnosing her problem—I can hardly complain if you're good enough to invite her to assist you in the shop.' The ultra-formal sentiments were softened by a rare, brief, sardonic smile; and Beth was surprised into returning it. 'And now,' he went on, getting to his feet and towering above her, 'I think you said you'd left young Amy in charge of your stockroom. Without disloyalty to my own offspring, I feel she shouldn't be abandoned to her own devices too much longer. God only knows what mischief she might get up to. You may not have discovered it yet, but she can be something of a scamp.'

Beth stood up too. 'Imaginative children usually can,' she agreed, glancing at her watch. 'Yes, you're right, we must get down there—I've got to open the shop, anyway. Thanks for saying she can do it. She'll be really pleased.'

He followed her through the door and down the stairs. 'I think I'm the one who should be grateful,' he remarked levelly.

Reaching the bottom, Beth turned and waited for him to catch up. 'And if she gets hungry while she's here—well, it would hardly be any skin off my nose if she has the odd snack would it?' she pointed out, her face straight but her eyes twinkling. 'I mean, I'm not going to care either way, am I?'

He took the point, and his air of faintly grudging respect deepened. 'Maybe you're right. It could be a breakthrough. Thanks again, Miss Porter. And . . .'

'Yes, Mr Franklyn?' she encouraged, as he hesitated, scanning her face.

'Someone with your education and intelligence is bound to realise that there's more to anorexia than simple loss of appetite. There are reasons, of course.' It was a quiet, definitive statement, offered without explanation or apology.

'I'd imagine there would be.' Her light tone assured him she wasn't pressing him on the point.

'You wouldn't upset her by probing too deeply into them, would you?' Paternal anxiety once and for all overcame that hard veneer, and it cracked to allow a gleam of real sensitivity to shine through.

'No, Mr Franklyn,' she asserted, 'I would not.'

'No. Pardon me for asking the question.' The apology was tense, but at least it showed a small degree of humility. 'We—I don't usually find outsiders taking such trouble . . . involving themselves in our affairs . . .'

For a change, his mastery of words was faltering, and Beth responded warmly to this hint of humanity. 'I quite understand. I wouldn't dream of mentioning it—to Amy or anyone else,' she assured him firmly. 'Now shall we join her? And don't forget,' she swung round, hit by an afterthought, and very nearly collided with him in the passageway, 'I was just asking your permission about her helping in the shop. If we don't make our story consistent and convincing, she's bound to come over suspicious.' Her voice was low but her expression sparked humour. 'And I for one wouldn't blame her.'

Then she continued on her way to the stockroom. Close behind her, Karl actually chuckled; and it was a heart-warming sound, reaching disconcertingly out to touch her at all sorts of levels. 'If we're into character analysis, Miss Porter,' he observed, 'I'd say it's just as well for my daughter she's enlisted you as an ally. It's my guess you'd make an exceedingly uncomfortable enemy.'

Beth kept her blushing cheeks facing well away from his range of vision. It was also just as well they'd arrived at the door of the stockroom, because she searched in vain for a suitably clever retort to this sudden parting of his defences. A few minutes later, her confusion was forgotten in the excitement of breaking the good news to Amy, and the girl's delight when she heard it.

But later, as she got ready for bed, she indulged in a few private musings over the day's events. It wasn't going to be all that easy, keeping her knowledge of Amy's anorexia to herself. And then there was that other Franklyn family secret she'd sworn to keep—even the man himself didn't know she was aware of his public identity. Instinctively she guessed he'd hate it if anyone knew, unless he saw fit to enlighten them. Perhaps one day—if her friendship with Amy was ever extended to include the rest of her family—her mother, for instance . . .?

No, she told herself, climbing gratefully in under her quilt. It wasn't going to be that kind of relationship. They were far too private and guarded for that. Where her dealings with Amy Franklyn were concerned, Beth was on her own.

CHAPTER THREE

IT had been a relentless sort of day; and it was a restless night. Her body was overtired, but her mind was overactive and her emotions overwrought—a fatal combination. Added to which, she had period cramps, a headache and a tickly throat, and she thought she was probably starting a cold.

At three she gave up the struggle to woo sleep, got up and made herself a hot drink, took two painkillers and settled down with the latest paperback romantic novel by one of her favourite writers. An hour later she fell into a fitful doze.

She slept late into a peaceful Sunday morning, blissfully lacking in alarm bells. She might have slept on even then, but at eleven she was plucked harshly into life by the buzz of her telephone. She stretched out a limp arm to grope for the receiver, blessing the day she'd had the foresight to get the private extension fitted in her bedroom.

'Hallo?' she mumbled sleepily into the earpiece.

'Lizzie?'

She lay back on the pillows, smiling and blinking, pushing the tangled mass of hair out of her eyes. Only one person was allowed to call her that, these days: her brother Andrew, three years her junior, still at home helping their parents to run the thriving family dairy farm. 'Drew! What's the idea, plaguing me at this unearthly hour?'

'Unearthly?' He was scandalised. 'I should say it's unearthly, if you're still in bed. I've been up since . . .'

'Yes, yes, I know all about that. Milking at six. Spare me the sob stuff. Some of us have things on our minds, and late nights. We don't all lead the simple bucolic life, you know.'

'Late nights? Things on your mind? Sounds fascinating. Can this be the serious, clean-living big sister who's such an example to us all?' His voice became a satirical imitation of a bad television linkman. 'The secret life of Beth Porter: does this quiet village bookstore-owner lead a double existence?'

She yawned. 'Don't be an idiot, Drew. I really was tired, and I think I'm starting a cold. Look, I'm supposed to be coming over for lunch. Did you want something before that? Is there a message from Mum or Dad?'

'Not really.' He sounded offended. 'Sorry if I broke in on your beauty sleep, Beth—and about your cold. You're not usually such a late bird. I didn't know.'

She instantly regretted her display of irritation. 'Of course you didn't. No, *I'm* sorry, Drew. I don't expect the cold will come to anything—I'm just a bit tired, that's all. I was just feeling grumpy.'

'That's okay.' He was his usual good-natured self at once. 'Sal and I just wondered if you'd feel like joining us for a drink before lunch? We'd like to see you on your own. It seems ages since we did, what with Sal off at college . . .'

Sally, the next sister down, had just completed teacher training and was back home looking for a job. 'What about Ma? Doesn't she need any help?'

'Apparently Paul's in charge of lunch today,' Andrew announced in tones of deep scepticism. 'Something to do with practising for O-level Home Economics.' He shuddered audibly. 'I did consider getting myself invited out, but Ma persuaded me to stay and show solidarity, and Pa said it was necessary to suffer in the cause of education—Paul's, that is—so I didn't.'

'I should think not. Paul's going to be a very good cook, which is more than you ever were,' she reminded him sternly. 'I'll look forward to it.'

'In my day,' Andrew pointed out, 'it was considered soft for boys to do Domestic Science. Woodwork,

metalwork or nothing it was, before these enlightened
times.'

'Then that's one way things have changed for the
better, these ten years,' Beth snapped—knowing he was
teasing, yet still half serious.

He chuckled. 'That's my Lizzie. Still the ardent
feminist even after a heavy night. Coming to the pub,
then? The Swan, we thought . . .'

'I'm not an ardent feminist, Drew. If you think I'm
ardent, or even a feminist, you haven't met a real
example of the species. Heaven help you if you do,' she
added darkly. 'I just think everyone's opportunities
should be equal, and that applies in both directions,
including boys learning about cooking and all that. And
yes, I'm coming to the pub, thank you very much, and
I'll see you there in an hour. Okay?' Now wide awake,
she sat on the edge of the bed, her bare feet searching
around underneath it for her slippers.

'I stand corrected on all counts.' She knew very well
that his meekness was as misleading as his chauvinistic
comments, and grinned. 'We'll look out for you at the
Swan, then—usual bar. I'll tell Ma we'll all be in
together at one.'

'Yes, do that. And Drew . . .'

'Yeah?'

'Thanks for asking me.'

'Don't be silly. It's ages since we all had a chat.
That's what families are there for.' He paused for a
moment. ''Bye, Beth.'

''Bye Drew. See you soon.'

It was good, of course, being part of a large,
supportive family—so close, both emotionally and
geographically. Beth knew how lucky she was. Perhaps
she tended to take it for granted, the way they were
there in the background when she needed someone.
Then again, she reflected as she got washed and
dressed, it did have some disadvantages too, as she'd
hinted to Amy only yesterday. You grew up learning to
trust people and confide in them, open yourself out to

them—and not all the people you went on to meet in the big world outside proved quite as caring and staunch as your own nearest and dearest.

As a young student she'd turned her back on them and fled to London—determined, quite naturally, to find independence and experience. She'd found plenty of both. But at the first threat of personal pain and strife she'd been back here like a shot. Admittedly she hadn't regretted it at all, but perhaps it had been a cop-out in some ways . . . she shook her head as she drank a cup of coffee. It wasn't the moment to work that one out.

Her sister and brother were waiting for her in the lounge bar of the pleasant country pub. They waved as she appeared and made her way through the Sunday crowds to join them, stopping here and there to exchange greetings with a familiar face.

'Bethy! Great to see you! You look lovely.' Sally, at twenty-one, was the more conventionally pretty of the two sisters—all red-brown curls, pert features, bright hazel eyes, rosebud mouth—though they shared the same trimly rounded build. But Beth's attraction was based on qualities which were more original and more enduring, if harder to define. There was an inner serenity, a kind of peace which emanated from her smooth skin, shining hair and deep dark eyes; and yet, in among it—part of its very fabric and yet separate like oil and water—a contrasting restlessness, a sensuality, an air of dissatisfaction. Sally was all surface brightness and warmth; Beth's reserve gave her a sense of mystery which intrigued a few people and frightened more away.

Both sisters were wearing slim-fitting cords and sweatshirts in autumnal shades. Beth grinned as she wondered fleetingly whether Sally unconsciously modelled herself on her older sister, or whether their mutual style came naturally to both. 'So do you, Sal, as always.' Beth perched herself on a high stool next to them. 'To be honest, I feel a bit washed out. Small dry sherry, please,' she told the hovering barman.

'You both look gorgeous to me,' Drew declared. 'No wonder I can't find a girl good enough. My standards are impossibly high with a pair of sisters like you. And even Lynne's shaping up better these days—losing some of that puppy fat.'

'Sexist.' Sally wrinkled her snub nose at him. 'You know no self-respecting girl would have you anyway.'

He groaned and clutched his forehead in mock despair. 'Not you and all! I'm surrounded by a monstrous regiment of women—liberated, to a man. You should hear Lynne going on at me—and she hasn't even left school yet.' He buried his glum face in his beermug.

Beth administered a comforting pat to her brother's stocky shoulder. He and Lynne were fair, solid and compact like their father, while the other three had inherited their mother's slighter frame and darker colouring. 'Never mind, poor old lad. Somewhere your other half surely awaits you.'

He emerged from his tankard, staring into it thoughtfully. 'Actually,' he informed her gravely, 'I've already had the full pint.'

Both women grimaced at this display of wit. 'He doesn't improve, does he?' Sally complained. 'I had hoped he might mature a little while I was away, but no such luck. It's all that communing with cows that does it. He could do with a bit of sophisticated company.'

'Like you two, you mean?' He snorted. 'I get better sense out of the yearlings. I've had a more erudite conversation,' he added pompously, 'with a haybale.'

They giggled and sipped their drinks. Such affectionate banter was all part of their relationship. Not only were they genuinely fond of each other, but they all had a real respect for each other's separateness. Being one of five, you learned to fight for your individuality if nothing else.

'On the subject of sophisticated company,' Sally remarked nonchalantly, examining a fingernail for rough edges, 'I've heard that one of our racier local boys is back in town after a spell in the big wide world.'

Her tone was deliberately offhand, but she avoided Beth's eyes, and the atmosphere seemed to grow unaccountably tense between them. Beth glanced at Andrew who chose that precise moment to drain his drink. 'Okay, so enlighten me.' Beth made an attempt at lightness of tone. 'No, wait a minute, let me guess . . . Gary Edwards?'

Sally laughed, and Andrew turned to his older sister with an expression of disbelief. The slight tension was broken. 'I said a spell in the big wide world, not a jail sentence,' Sally reminded her. 'Anyway, if I'm right, Gary still has at least a year to serve.'

'She said sophisticated company, not criminal expertise,' Andrew contributed to the discussion. 'The man she has in mind may not be renowned for his honest dealings . . .' he hesitated, glancing at Beth, then apparently decided to see the thing through, 'but sophisticated he certainly always was.'

'Probably even more so now,' Sally endorsed, 'after all these years.'

Beth's mind already knew perfectly well who they meant. Only one person fitted their description; only one name would have them both looking at her, yet trying not to look at her, with that expression of protective concern in their faces. Whatever they were trying to tell her—had doubtless brought her here specially to warn her—they were being unusually tactful and cautious about it.

'You don't have to make it easy for me.' She gulped down her sherry and looked about for the barman. She never had more than one drink on an empty stomach, but suddenly she felt an overwhelming need for fortification. 'I can take it—I'd rather know, if it's who I think it is. Come on, let's have it.'

Their silence confirmed it. Neither of them could bear to vocalise his name, knowing how he'd kicked holes in Beth's life. They'd asked her here with the express purpose of breaking the news to Beth—and now they'd got to the point, they couldn't do it. If it wasn't so appalling, it might have been funny.

Beth took a long breath and saved them the trouble. 'Are you, by any chance, talking about Nicholas Hallett?' she suggested—her voice low but steady—clearly audible only to them among the mercifully noisy throng.

Two faces turned at once in her direction, studies in anxious relief. 'Oh Beth!' Sally sighed. 'I wish you didn't have to know, but you might so easily bump into him, and I don't know how long he's staying, or why he's here, or exactly where . . .'

Now that the subject had been broached, Andrew found his normal articulacy. 'Somewhere in Falconden, I was told, or near. We thought we should let you know—if you didn't already. You didn't, did you, Liz?' he pressed, his light grey eyes on her face.

'No. At least . . .' Why was she hesitating, when she hadn't had the least idea? Had something given her a hint or a clue—some subliminal sighting of him round a corner—some mention of his name in the shop? Whatever the reason, the shock of this discovery seemed dulled, as if she'd been thinking about him recently without realising it—as if her own memory had dredged him out of his hiding place of its own accord, by some supernatural process . . .

'No,' she assured them more firmly, 'I didn't know. Thanks for telling me.' She smiled at them both so that they could see how calmly she was taking it. 'I'm really grateful to you for telling me. It was absolutely the right thing to do. Now I'll be prepared, if I do see him—and with any luck, I won't have to.'

Sensing that Beth had no wish to pursue the subject but needed a few minutes alone with her thoughts, Sally and Andrew were soon immersed in superficial chat. But Beth's quick mind was ranging busily over past events, both very recent and long distant, now merging strangely together. This was it—she was on the point of grasping it—the missing link.

Nick Hallett. Inevitably the name conjured up the face: blonde, good-looking, blue-eyed, bursting with youthful charm; extrovert, irresistible ... and that face immediately conjured up another, younger face: pale, innocent, inward-drawn—and yet somehow an echo of his own. Amy Franklyn.

This was the message her brain had been feverishly working on these last few days and nights. This was the connection she'd fought, and yet dreaded, to make. Each time she'd looked at Amy, some obscure corner of her mind had been painfully made aware of Nick. But why? Why? Forcing herself to stay calmly rational, now that she'd had to face the realisation at last, Beth went through the possibilities.

The uncanny physical resemblance certainly seemed striking, if she was honest. Those angelic fair curls, the shape of the face, even the limpid expression—intensely feminine on the girl, it had nonetheless suited the young man equally well, or so Beth had considered at the time ... she hugged herself, biting her lip to recall that beautiful face, and the beautiful body that had gone with it, and the far-from-beautiful heart hidden inside.

Then there were Amy's volatile moods: the quicksilver shifts from stubborn depression to contagious charm; the pouts, the wide smiles, the winning ways. Amy was only a schoolgirl and she'd grow out of all that adolescent unpredictability—in fact, apart from her unfortunate problem, she already showed signs of maturing fast. But Beth now knew that she'd seen an older, male version of all that before. And Nick had been a grown man, with claims to poise and confidence and sexual experience. Perhaps he'd had time to grow up a bit by now. In any case, Beth had no intention of finding out.

No; the whole thing must be one of those odd coincidences which happen from time to time. There was no way the young girl—a visitor to the village,

child of a famous Canadian author—could be connected
to the man who'd been born and bred right here. Their
faces and mannerisms were similar, that was all. Now
that she'd solved the mystery, Beth could forget all
about it. She took another sip of her second sherry, and
allowed her memory to wander freely, rarely, over those
dramatic days. Another world, it seemed now, from the
safety of this moment.

Nick Hallett was two years older than Beth, but all
the way through school he had glowed like a gorgeous
golden god—remote, unattainable, impossibly delectable. She'd admired him from afar from the first year to
the fifth; and then he'd left, disappeared into the morass
of the metropolis to seek his fortune while she worked
her way steadily through the sixth form to university.

By the time she was stuck into her new life in
London—blossoming out among her books, developing
her new talent for selling them—she'd forgotten all
about him. And then one night, during a visit home,
she'd bumped into him at a party given by an old
school friend in a neighbouring village. And much to
her amazement, this idol of her childhood days had
taken one look at her across the crowded room—and
made a dead set in her direction.

Halcyon college days and nearly two years as proud
owner of a successful shop had boosted Beth's self-
respect and confidence; but she still couldn't begin to
make out why Nick Hallett should decide to show such
a blatant interest in her—here, now, after so long. She
glared at him suspiciously as he approached, as
unbearably sexy as ever in tight denims and smart
leather bomber jacket, his blonde hair curling as
attractively as it always had around his sharp, regular
features, his eyes as blue and clear as she remembered
them.

'Hi there, Beth.' You'd have thought they'd been the
closest of buddies rather than fellow-pupils of several
years ago, who never even used to speak to each other.
'Good to see you back at the ranch. How's it going?'

Then, before she'd found a suitably cool reply, he'd reached out and grabbed her, murmuring 'Dance?' as he whisked her smoothly away—obviously assuming it would never enter her head to refuse.

The sensations which flooded through Beth at this sudden closeness to Nick Hallett—a situation she'd willingly have given her whole collection of Beatle posters to be in, some ten years back—were all but overpowering. But she collected her dignity, held herself aloof and stared him in the eye. 'I'm okay,' she assured him politely. 'How's life treating you?'

'Fine.' His hold on her tightened, and he laid his cheek against hers, which made further conversation difficult, to say the least.

'What are you up to these days?' she enquired as soon as he let her up for air.

'Oh, this and that,' he replied vaguely. 'Drink?' he'd invited as the music came to an end; and taking her proprietorially by the hand he'd led her to the table which groaned under its weight of bottles. Then he'd proceeded to ply her with alcohol as if there'd been no tomorrow.

Puzzled but flattered by his attentions, Beth had allowed herself to go under without too much of a struggle. His endearing qualities had only increased with age, she decided. There couldn't be any harm in riding along with this rather delicious tide which had so unexpectedly swept her up, could there?

'A little bird tells me,' he was murmuring teasingly in her ear, after her fourth glass of white wine, 'that you're running your own business, and very well too. Is that right?'

His voice and expression indicated that a girl so young and lovely couldn't, surely, be successful in the hard world of commerce; and not surprisingly, Beth rose straight to the bait. 'It certainly is,' she'd assured him with careful emphasis. 'Books. I sell books. And,' she grinned happily, 'lots of people buy them.'

He'd leaned over her, his blue eyes warm with

admiration, and planted a chaste kiss on her inviting cheek. Then he'd retreated to a respectful distance while he continued to gaze soulfully at her. 'All the brains, and beauty too,' he'd muttered intensely. 'Some ladies have all the luck.'

For once in her short sensible life, Beth had allowed charming compliments to go to her head. After all, it wasn't as if he was a stranger or anything like that; they weren't ten miles from where they'd both been born, surrounded by mutual acquaintances, safe within the confines of home territory. London was where you met the wolves and con-men, where dangers lay all around. This was different.

For the rest of the evening she revelled in his company and the envious glances of other girls, flirting outrageously back when he chatted her up, eagerly returning his ardent but respectful embraces when the lights went down for the last couple of hours' dancing. As she tore herself away to be transported home on Cloud Nine (in the shape of Andrew's old banger of a van), Nick stole one last, long, lingering kiss; and it was the most passionate, the most arousing kiss she'd ever been given. From that second she was utterly, irrevocably hooked.

'Can I look you up when we're back in London?' he'd pleaded softly, obviously in a turmoil of impatience, nuzzling his shining head into her warm neck, nibbling her earlobe so that her breath caught in her throat.

'Why not?' Dazed, whirling and spinning with delight, she could find nothing but good in the suggestion. The whole occasion was, in fact, too good to be real. 'Give me a ring at home tomorrow,' she'd whispered, 'and I'll give you my address.'

He had; and she did. And within a week he was on the doorstep of her shop, as vibrantly attractive as ever, reporting for the next stage in their double-act.

He'd sauntered in, hands in pockets, and gazed admiringly round the well-ordered, prosperous little scene. 'Hey, Beth—this is great! Great! What an achievement!' He whistled gently through his teeth, and even that turned her already captive heart over. 'You're a clever girl, you know that? As well as—all the rest,' he added meaningfully.

She'd blushed and denied it, but all the same she'd glowed with pleasure at his praise. For the next few weeks he was her constant escort and companion. He involved himself at all levels of her life, popping into her shop at all hours of the day, making himself at home in her flat at all hours of the night, taking over her private and social life until he was its centre, its core and its only focus.

Her cherished independence disappeared over the horizon in a rosy cloud. Nick was all and everything to her. When a woman like Beth Porter—self-contained, shy, cautious, but full of romantic longings—finally takes the plunge, she takes it all the way. And when Beth let go, she really let go.

When he wasn't expertly courting her—gradually tantalising her to a peak of need and adoration so that she'd be ripe for seduction—Nick was in the shop, casually adopting the business as his own. Blinded by love, she hardly took in the fact that he seemed to spend remarkably little time following his own career—which was, he assured her, teaching in an English Language school, at which he claimed to be making a tidy living, though it didn't seem to involve many hours a week. But the more time he chose to spend with Beth, the better she liked it, and she wasn't complaining. She went on tending the shop and doing very nicely, building up the profits. In the evenings they went out together—or even better, stayed in together; and she cooked dinner for them both; and life was perfect.

When she finally, ecstatically, gave herself to him, he'd set the stage meticulously so that the whole occasion seemed natural and inevitable and right. And perhaps, on one level, it was. Physically, she never regretted making that ultimate commitment. She was in love, and she thought he was; and after all, those were the main ingredients of a successful affair, weren't they?

At the time, of course, she'd assumed it was more than just a temporary affair. She'd been wrong; but it wasn't any less exciting for all that, opening her up to new sensations and experiences which she'd craved, unwittingly, for years. Yes, she had that to thank Nick for, and she didn't hold it against him—not now, after all this time when hindsight lent wisdom. She'd been easy prey; begging for it.

The trouble was, you couldn't seal off those newly-exposed pathways as if they'd never been trampled. You were never the same afterwards; only more guarded and wary—and unwilling to risk it all over again, whatever happened.

No, it hadn't been the sexual side of her relationship with Nick which had proved so painful and disastrous. It had been the emotional side—or rather, the fact that on his part, as it turned out, there never *was* an emotional side. While she'd been glorying in the pangs of first love, he'd been cold-bloodedly softening her up; and she'd been too blinkered to see it, for all her intelligence. That practised eye had lit on her at the party—vulnerable, virginal creature as she so patently was; and his sharp ear had picked up the information from the grapevine about her outstandingly successful business enterprise . . . and he'd followed his predatory instinct from that point, moving in for the kill. In order to get his hands on her profits, it had been necessary to get his feet well and truly under her table and his head on her pillow.

Nick Hallett had achieved all three without any problem, and no doubt enjoyed every moment of it. It wasn't the first time he'd set out to make a killing, and it wasn't destined to be the last. In fact, before he'd even had a chance to move in and actually make use of his tight hold on Beth's small but growing capital, he'd met another, more challenging victim. Older, riper, richer pickings in the form of a faded widow who seized

eagerly on this godlike young gift—grabbing the chance
of youth revisited, not to mention the status symbol,
the boost to her ego—and bore him away to help her
spend her considerable wealth.

Beth stood sadly by and watched him go. What else
could she do? She was a realist as well as a romantic,
and one part of her had probably guessed it was
coming. Hadn't she warned herself, way back at the
party, that it was all too good to be real? Perhaps she
ought to have listened to herself, but regrets served no
purpose. It was over and done now, woven into life's
rich tapestry.

But another part of her was deeply shattered, and it
was by far the most important part. Her body would
get over the shock, her bruised heart would heal in
time. The worst pain was the blow to her faith in
human nature, and above all in her own pride, her
judgment. She was the craziest, most pathetic fool to
have trusted him in the first place. How could she have
been so naïve as not to spot his true motives?

For a month or so she buried herself in hard work,
apparently remarkably unscathed. Then reaction set
in—quite suddenly, overnight—and she crumbled into
acute nervous anxiety. Fighting off stress, keeping it
submerged, only causes it to surface all the more
violently in the end; and Beth found this out the hard
way. Her shop, her flat, everything around her became
hateful. London became hell. All she wanted was to get
away, flee the scene of her corruption and degradation;
make for the shelter of familiar territory—home.

Within three months she'd purchased a good site
which happened to be for sale in the High Street of
Falconden—and after that she'd hardly looked back.
Three years later—older and slightly wiser—of course
she knew she'd had a narrow escape. Nick had
plundered her virtue and her confidence, but at least
he'd left her intact professionally. Starry-eyed as she'd
been, she doubted now whether she'd even have noticed
once he started helping himself to her profits—

wheedling his way further and deeper into the business, taking her over lock, stock and bookshelf . . . and that, she was now convinced, was all he'd had in mind right from the outset. She winced whenever she thought of it, and drew her tight little cocoon more securely round her.

Yes, she'd been let off lightly. She thanked the fates for sending the rich widow along just when they did. Occasionally, snippets of news about Nick reached her. He'd left the widow within a year—no doubt a profligate, riotous year; gone off to America, where he was rumoured to be thriving. His parents had died, but he hadn't put in an appearance at either funeral. He'd become a singer, it was reported; an actor . . . a banker . . . married into an illustrious family . . . stories flew about but Beth knew better than to take any notice of them.

And now, according to Sally and Andrew, who usually knew these things, he was back. Was he looking for her? Did he even know she was living here now? Had he returned to flaunt his transatlantic riches in front of old friends, or to haunt old flames, or simply on a family visit? Did he, for that matter, still have any family left in these parts? Beth wasn't at all sure that he did; she hadn't heard of any Halletts for a long time— not since his mother had died.

Whatever the reasons for his appearance, she could only hope it had nothing to do with her, and that their paths wouldn't cross. Draining her drink, she held her head high and smiled at her sister and brother. 'Isn't it time we were off?' Her voice was steady, her eyes calm as she glanced at the clock on the wall. 'We don't want Paul's meal to spoil.'

Two warm smiles came back to her at once. 'Right.' Sally wriggled down off her stool. 'He was very particular about everyone sitting down on time.'

Behind them, as they left the bar, Andrew could be heard muttering darkly, 'O-level Home Economics, forsooth. What a guy needs after a hard week's work is a good square Sunday dinner.'

On the way across the car park, his two sisters linked arms with him—the older on one side, the younger on the other. 'You'll get your square meal, Drew. You'll be surprised. Ma will have been keeping an eye from a tactful distance. You don't think she'd let her baby poison the rest of the family, do you?' Sally reassured him.

'She wouldn't let her firstborn son and chief labourer starve to death, either,' pointed out Beth caustically.

Andrew wasn't that easily mollified, however. 'I'll believe it when I taste it.' He shuffled his feet gloomily. 'Remember that macaroni cheese he brought home? Like putty, it was. You could have pointed the brickwork with it. Even the hens wouldn't touch it.'

'Andrew,' Beth reproved him sternly, 'you have no family loyalty.'

'Oh yes I have. I just have an empty stomach as well, that's all.' He broke away from them to unlock his battered van. 'See you back there then?' He turned to Sally. 'I expect you'd rather ride in Beth's posh carriage than this old bus?'

'I'd hardly call my baby Fiat a posh carriage,' Beth observed, fishing for her keys in her handbag.

'Since you're in such a miserable old mood, I'd better come with you and cheer you up.' Sally grinned at Beth as she climbed sedately in beside her brother. 'I'm not having you depressing Paul and the parents with your gloom and doom.'

As it turned out, the meal was excellent: hot, tasty and professionally served. Andrew was forced to eat his words along with two platefuls of roast beef, Yorkshire pudding and vegetables, followed by plum pie. Paul basked in the light of their approval. 'I think I might be a chef,' he pronounced thoughtfully.

'You just concentrate on getting those GCEs first,' Val Porter reminded him fondly.

'That's okay Mum.' He smiled at her—a bright, cheerful boy who held life in the palm of his hand. 'I'll get them, don't worry. Then I'll go to Paris and train with one of the top men there.'

Joe Porter raised his bushy brows. 'Paris, eh?' He grinned expansively round at his assembled family—the proud patriarch, an educated man of agricultural stock who had returned to the land after trying out a number of other occupations. 'Well, why not, eh?'

'Why not indeed?' Beth smiled back at him, already mellowed by their undemanding company, the good food, several glasses of strong cider.

By the end of the afternoon, chatting quietly to her mother and sisters in front of the fire, she'd relaxed so much that she'd almost forgotten today's disturbing piece of news; not to mention the other new twists which had suddenly entered her life.

Almost; but not entirely. As she drove the eight miles or so home, through the smoky dusk of an early autumn evening, they came flooding back into her mind. Amy; and Nick; and Karl. Were they all parts of the same complex pattern—and if so, how? She shook her head, as if to clear away cobwebs. She was very tired, and it was making her give way to whims and fancies. And that was something she never, ever did.

CHAPTER FOUR

AMY reported for duty at ten next morning, frail as ever but bright-eyed and raring to go. Apart from anything else, Beth surmised, the girl had obviously been bored. She bit back fussy queries about whether or not Amy had had any breakfast, contenting herself with a smile of greeting.

'Hallo Amy. You do look smart this morning. You'll raise the tone of the old place just by being here.'

Amy took off her coat and glanced down at her blue flared skirt with the pretty patch pockets and matching blouse. 'Am I too dressed up, d'you think?' The drawn young features, faintly flushed from fresh autumn air, creased in uncertainty. 'I don't often wear a skirt, but I thought, well—you know—meeting the public . . .'

Beth's heart contracted a little in affectionate response. She remembered too well what it was like to be that age and perpetually unsure of whether one was doing, wearing or saying the right thing. 'Not in the least,' she assured Amy emphatically. 'You look just right, and I appreciate it that you've made the effort, and I know the customers will too.'

Amy's relief was transparent. She came to join Beth, standing with thin legs apart and hands shoved well into her pockets. 'So, what do I do first?'

'Well—we're not too busy yet. How about getting to grips with the children's section for me? I haven't had time to change it for ages, and there's a whole pile of new books and pictures for display, just waiting to be arranged.'

'Sure. Sure I will. Boy, just leave it to me—you won't be able to keep 'em away once I've finished over there.' Amy set to with a will, and more than a touch of flair.

Beth supervised from a discreet distance, admiring the girl's application and concentration, again marvelling at the way adult and child could be so strongly mixed together in the one unformed frame.

At lunchtime they shut up shop and went up to the flat. Once again, Amy refused vehemently even to contemplate food, and Beth took it in her stride, simply carrying on with making her own snack. But this time Amy stayed reasonably calm, though distinctly tense; and this time, when Beth produced the toasted cheese from under the grill—golden-brown and melting, filling the kitchen with its tantalising savoury smell—Amy's defences crumbled, as Beth had hoped they might.

'Maybe,' she muttered sheepishly, staring down at her hands, 'maybe I might just manage a small piece of that. If you've really got enough. I seem to be kinda peckish after all, and it looks real good.'

'Of course there's enough; anyway I can always make some more.' Matter-of-fact, without so much as a glance in Amy's direction, Beth put the two slices on to small plates, added half a tomato to each and pushed one across the table to Amy. Then she turned her back on the girl, busying herself with kettle and teapot, instinctively guessing that Amy would prefer not to be watched over as she ate.

By the time she sat down and began on her own slice, her young guest had demolished the first half and was licking her fingers appreciatively. Beth chatted aimlessly as she ate, feigning complete uninterest as Amy got through the second piece with equal enjoyment. Afterwards they shared a pot of tea, and Beth set a bowl of fruit on the table between them, absent-mindedly taking an apple and biting into it as she explained the mysteries of VAT, bemoaning the fact that she had to spend so much time filling in forms and adding up figures.

Although she made no sign, she knew perfectly well that Amy's eyes were fixed longingly on the bunch of firm bananas which nestled among the rest of the fruit.

For five full minutes she ogled them, her blue eyes round; then she cracked. A skinny arm snaked towards the bowl, a bony hand snapped one off and peeled it, sharp white teeth attacked it eagerly.

Taking no notice, Beth went on talking animatedly, chewing her apple, apparently forgetting all about Amy's declarations of disgust about food in general. But when Amy had finished every bite of her banana, she risked a glance at the girl's face, and was shocked at its expression: a complex study in triumph and guilt, shame and defiance. Certainly this tiny meal for a normal person was a giant step for a severe anorexic. Equally certainly, Amy had a long way to go yet before her mind could allow her body to accept sustenance without fear or anger. In her own home, Beth suspected, even this small amount would rarely, if ever, pass her lips.

During the afternoon, fortified by this unusual nourishment, Amy settled to her tasks as if she'd been born to them. When Beth allowed her to deal direct with a customer—taking the money for a couple of greetings cards—she was as good as her word: a portrait of gentility and charm. Beth stifled a smile, recalling the petulant child she already knew so well as the other side of that same coin.

At four o'clock some youngsters burst in on the peace and quiet, heading for the children's section where they spotted the new displays at once. Amy was delighted, and spent a happy hour encouraging them as they browsed, pointing out books they might like, even reading passages from some favourites to the smaller ones. Beth raised her eyebrows and went on serving the adult customers. At this rate Amy was going to prove indispensable, easily giving as much help as she was getting. And no one seemed to find it at all odd that Beth's new assistant was so young. Perhaps they guessed there was a personal story behind Amy's sudden presence; in any case they accepted it happily, and Beth warmed to them for it.

By five-thirty the children had all left for their tea and the shop was empty. Beth went to the door to lock it and turn the notice round, yawning and stretching. 'That was quite a day,' she remarked. 'You've been wonderful, Amy. An asset.'

Amy's face lit up. 'Really? You really mean it? You're not just saying it?'

'Of course I mean it.' Beth began tidying up her desk. 'I don't say things I don't mean. One day you'll believe that.' She smiled. 'I hope you've enjoyed it, too?'

Amy's expression spoke her answer much plainer than any words. 'I loved it, Beth. You know I did. Can I come every day?'

'As long as it's okay at home, you can come as often as you like. I only hope,' she added on a wry note, 'I won't forget how I ever managed without you.' She looked out at the fast-gathering dusk. It was depressing, the way it fell so early these November days. 'Now, shouldn't you be getting off home before it gets any darker? Or shall we have a cup of tea and then I can drive you back?'

'Oh no, you don't have to do that. Dad said I wasn't to be a nuisance. He's coming to fetch me. He should be here any time. He doesn't want me out alone after dark,' she explained—her tone suggesting that grownups were all the same, fussing over silly things.

'I see.' Busy locking up the till, Beth wondered why this piece of casual information should make her stiffen. Of course the careful father would want to make sure his only daughter got home safely. It was only to be expected.

All day, mindful of her promise to Karl, she'd kept conversation steadily away from anything too personal, avoiding mention of Amy's family, or her past, or any subject which might prove disturbing or problematic. It hadn't been too difficult, since there was plenty going on, and anyway Beth wasn't particularly inquisitive by nature; and Amy had certainly loosened up visibly under the influence of this undemanding new friendship.

Some of the time, Beth had even forgotten exactly who the girl was—or rather who her father was—and the general air of uneasy mystery which surrounded them both. As she got to know Amy better, to see her for the person she really was, Beth found that earlier sense of unpleasant familiarity fading fast. Obviously there had been nothing significant in it—just one of those curious, inexplicable quirks of the subconscious; nothing to brood over.

Now she braced herself for another confrontation with Karl; and he duly appeared at the door of her flat ten minutes later, coat collar turned up against a brisk evening breeze, car keys jangling in one gloved hand. His gaze, keen and sharp, probed Beth's face and then strayed behind her in search of Amy; but the rest of his countenance was as withdrawn, as detached as ever.

Beth's automatic reaction was to freeze into an equally guarded, defensive mask. But all at once, as she faced him, she found herself relaxing into a smile of genuine welcome. It was impossible not to respond to that open, tender concern he showed for his daughter. Since Beth not only understood it but shared it, this mutual aloofness, hostility even, seemed out of place. Surely the mature thing to do was to accept the man, moody and difficult as he undoubtedly was, with her usual good-natured serenity—not fight him off, as some deeper instinct still urged her to do?

'Hallo there,' she greeted him, her tone light and friendly. 'Won't you come in? Amy's just popped upstairs to the bathroom but she'll be down in a few minutes. She's all ready for you.' She stepped back; but he didn't move.

'How's it been?' he barked—never one to beat about the bush, as she knew well enough by now.

'Please come in,' she repeated more firmly, hugging her soft brown wool sweater closely round her. Arrested by the gesture, his eyes travelled down her body—at once abstracted, unseeing, yet clearly taking in every curve and detail. 'You're letting all my lovely warm air escape,' she complained mildly.

His eyes sparked but he inclined his tousled dark head slightly. 'I apologise, Miss Porter. Thoughtless of me.' He stepped inside and pushed the door to behind him until it clicked shut. Then he tried again. 'Now, how's it . . .'

'Beth,' she interrupted sweetly. If terse toughness was his only method of communication, that didn't mean it had to be hers as well.

'Pardon me?' One heavy eyebrow lifted as he registered her amendment.

But she wasn't to be daunted so easily. 'My name is Beth. Please,' she elaborated graciously, as he still appeared nonplussed, 'won't you call me Beth? Mr Franklyn,' she added—staring him straight in the eyes, defiant, humorous, satirical almost as she tagged his own surname on to the end of her polite invitation.

For a moment he returned the stare, unflinching, and she thought she'd made him angry with her threat to his formal defences. Then the stern features yielded to a grin; and it was a revelation, a transformation which all but took Beth's precious poise clean away. Like that unexpected chuckle, two days ago, which had sliced through his brusque manner like a hot knife through cold butter. Totally disarming.

'Fair enough.' The grin widened, and it reached his eyes. 'Perhaps you're right—since you appear to have successfully made a takeover bid for my daughter, maybe we shouldn't stand on ceremony.'

'Oh, I hope I haven't done that,' she protested—faintly shocked at such an accusation. 'Mr Franklyn,' she added again, meaningfully.

He took the point. 'Karl,' he corrected, again with that slight inclination of the head towards her. 'If you're Beth,' he asserted, grey eyes glittering, 'then I must be Karl. Okay?'

'Okay,' she agreed meekly, hoping her face wasn't giving away the shock waves she was feeling at the sound of her name coming so easily from his lips. After all, she'd instructed him to use it.

He leaned against the wall now, hands thrust casually into pockets, surveying her with a good deal more frank interest and a good deal less tension. She'd broken through a layer of ice—or perhaps it was protective glass; that was something, she supposed, though the process had cost her more than he could have suspected. 'So—Beth.' Again she struggled to hide the frisson which unaccountably shook her. 'May I now enquire, with due deference and decorum, how the day has progressed here at your shop? *Vis-à-vis* my daughter,' he expanded, with mock pomposity. 'Has she behaved herself, or has she got under your feet in the worst way? Are you,' he relaxed as the wordsmith took over, finally banishing that tough screen of caution, 'regretting your offer already?'

She shook her head vehemently, glaring round and up to see whether Amy was in the offing. 'It's been great, actually. She's been a real help, just as I thought she'd be—and I've enjoyed her company.' She kept her tone calm and level, but there was just a hint of '*so there!*' underlining the words.

His expression showed relief, and no small surprise. 'No kidding?'

'It couldn't have gone better. I hope you'll let her come in every day—whenever she wants. I'm absolutely sure it's . . . what she needs.'

His gaze followed hers up the stairs. There was no sign of Amy yet. He opened his mouth to say something, then closed it again—frowning, apparently battling briefly with himself. Then, as if reaching a decision, he took a step towards her so that he was alarmingly close, and demanded, his voice low but intense: 'Did she eat anything today, Beth?'

Beth had known this was coming, but she'd deliberately waited to see if he'd raise the subject. Now she nodded as confidently as she could with those troubled grey eyes searching her gentle brown ones from only just above her. 'Yes.'

'She did?' Again, disbelief mingled with delight in his expression.

'She did—a bit more this time. Some cheese on toast. Half a tomato. Tea, with milk and sugar. And,' she smiled slightly, 'a banana.' It was like calorie-counting, only for the opposite reasons, noting down every morsel, every mouthful.

He was watching her as she spoke, and his smile reflected hers, his eyes glinting. 'A ban*arn*a? H*arf* a tom*art*o?' he echoed, aping her very English pronunciation.

'Okay then,' she retorted with spirit, her own eyes gleaming. 'H*a'f* a tom*ay*to. Call it what you like, that's what she ate for lunch.'

'Forgive me, Beth.' In this new atmosphere of honesty between them, he was as unpredictable as his daughter. Now he became solemn and contrite. 'That was rude of me. After all, I'm the foreigner in these parts. I just couldn't help it. I love to hear an English accent—especially,'—was she imagining it, or did his face darken for an instant?—'in a woman.'

She was more than ready for that one. 'And I'm not averse to American and Canadian ones,' she informed him, with equal gravity, 'even in a man.'

For a split second he seemed put out; then he burst into laughter—a rich, wholehearted sound which filled up the space around them and penetrated far into Beth's private space as well. '*Touché, touché*, Miss Porter.' His brows knitted thoughtfully as he recovered his composure. 'Like I said, you'd make a ferocious enemy. God help the man who's fool enough—or brave enough—to spar with you.'

A silence hung between them, perhaps for ten seconds, which seemed to hum with unspoken communications; and yet it was strangely peaceful. Then Beth cleared her throat and forced her gaze to unlock from his. There was a sound of a door slamming upstairs, and energetic young footsteps heading along a corridor above them.

Karl started out of his dreamy perusal of Beth's face, as if sharply aware of a conversation left unfinished. reaching out one hand to grab her sleeve—his eyes now urgent, piercing on hers. 'Thanks, Beth.' It was a murmur, hardly more than a whisper; but the intensity of the words and the action, the burning touch of his fingers on her arm, caused her to jump back as if he'd bellowed at the top of his voice.

He released her and moved away as Amy appeared at the top of the stairs and began thundering down them as if she weighed seventeen stone rather than barely seven. Beth's quiet 'That's all right, Karl,' was all but lost under her exuberant shouts of 'Hi, Dad!', and 'Guess what I did today?'

Karl opened his arms to greet his high-spirited adolescent with a bear-hug. The warmth in his face as he smiled at Beth over the top of the shining blonde curls did more than words ever could to show his gratitude. Mesmerised by the sight, she could only smile back and shrug, indicating how glad she'd been to do it.

'See you tomorrow, Beth?' Pausing on the way out, one hand tucked into the safety of her father's arm, Amy allowed her tone to betray just a hint of anxiety.

Just a hint; but it wasn't lost on Beth's sensitive ear. 'You bet—I'm counting on you. But make sure you're feeling strong,' she warned. 'I've hardly got you started yet. Once I really get you going, you won't know what's hit you.'

Amy wasn't taken in for a moment by this display of autocracy, and laughed happily. Beth waved as the man and the girl walked down the road to their car.

The next few days followed much the same pattern; and it was a pattern which changed the basic shape of Beth's life. Amy soon gave up even pretending to refuse the snack she was offered at midday; and each time, with increasing confidence and decreasing anxiety, she ate a little more. Beth watched in silent pleasure, but never said a word, knowing that might spoil everything.

In the shop, Amy took her duties very seriously; and

it was all Beth could do to persuade her to take an hour off, perhaps to sit quietly in the stockroom, or in a corner of the shop itself, with a book. Her enthusiasm was delightful, of course, and surely beneficial to her in the long run; but she was still not strong. The last thing Beth wanted to do was exhaust her physically in the process of building her up emotionally.

Still keeping strictly to her resolution, Beth never drew the girl out about her private life or problems, just as Amy never volunteered any information. But Beth could hardly help forming her own suspicions on the subject. After that very first day, when Amy had commented on their relative ages, she'd never once mentioned her mother. Her father came every evening to fetch her home, without fail; but there was no sign, no suggestion, of anyone waiting for them there. In the brief chats which he and Beth exchanged, there was no hint at the existence of a wife.

Gradually, rather than overnight, Beth began to admit to herself that no Mrs Karl Franklyn appeared to be in evidence. Whoever and wherever she might be, Amy's mother was not part of her everyday life; and unless Beth's usual intuition had deserted her, this fact almost certainly had a lot to do with Amy's general depletion of body and spirit.

Lying awake at night, at last letting her thoughts range freely over these absorbing possibilities, Beth found herself torn in all kinds of new directions. How could she feel anything but intense pity and sorrow for the sweet, sad girl who was—whether temporarily or permanently—bereft of her mother? On the other hand, there was a sharp tremor of irrational excitement in the merest suspicion that Karl Franklyn lived alone. At least, without a wife. At least, at the moment. Beth reminded herself, very sensibly, several times, that these people were strangers to her; that she knew nothing about them until they themselves were ready to tell her more.

But it was a losing battle. Her heart was apparently

declaring unilateral independence from her head; and it was creeping into life under the powerful combined influence of Amy and her father—warming up, thawing out like a small creature emerging from hibernation. And there wasn't a damn thing the rest of her could do about it—even if it wanted to; which, on the whole, it didn't.

By the weekend she was in a state of heightened awareness of everything. The world seemed more intense in every way, the colours brighter, the air sharper, despite November greyness. Yet there was another dimension in which she felt removed from reality, trance-like. She went through daily life with her usual placid efficiency, and no one—least of all Karl or Amy—would have noticed the difference; but inside she seethed with new energies, swelled with a new vitality, like a kite tugging on the end of its string, pulled and beckoned by huge winds and endless skies.

Perhaps it was inevitable that the brief contact she had with Karl every evening should become a focal point of her life. After his initial curt barriers had been broken down, giving way to that easy, vibrant warmth, she found herself looking forward to seeing him all day. He remained intensely grateful for her practical involvement in Amy—surprised, even, that anyone outside the family should take so much trouble over someone else's problem. When Amy was there, of course, he could hardly make open enquiries into what she'd eaten that day. By mutual, unspoken consent, the topic was never raised in her presence. But he'd always signal the question to Beth with a twitch of a brow, a twist of the long mouth; and she'd nod her reassurance firmly, just once; and he'd smile his comprehension.

It seemed to Beth that their communications were packed with an understanding, an empathy which was little short of alarming. Certainly she'd never experienced anything quite like it before. At the same time, he was still a law unto himself—volatile, unpredictable; and his moods affected her own far more deeply than they had any right to. It probably only depended, she told herself severely, on how his work had gone that day—assuming, since she was officially ignorant of its true nature and couldn't really ask, that he was currently occupied in writing another book. But the undeniable fact remained: when he was direct, witty and relaxed, the rays stretched on for hours and lit up her evening; and when he was terse, difficult and tense, she felt bleak and on edge most of the night.

And all this time, as the days merged together into a blur of activity and emotion, she never heard any more about Nick Hallett. Perhaps Sally and Andrew had made a mistake—a twist in the grapevine, a fault on the line. In any case, he certainly hadn't drifted into Beth's field of vision, and she was only too glad to let herself believe he wasn't going to. Her dear sister and brother had had her best interests at heart—but for once, they or their informant had got it wrong.

It was amazingly easy to push those recently-stirred memories of Nick right back into the outer regions of her mind, where they belonged. They had no place in her thoughts now; she preferred not to be reminded of yesterday's foolishness today. She'd grown up since, into a mature person. She'd learned her lesson; those headstrong, romantic days were over.

Then why, her mind nagged unkindly, filling her head in those dark small hours, did she look to be in imminent danger of going under all over again? She was, it pointed out, doing rather a good imitation of a woman on the brink of falling in love—falling far and fast, just as she had on that earlier occasion. And this time the man, though admittedly in a different league from Nick, was surely no more suitable or promising or conducive?

She attempted to silence her mind with a few well-chosen words; but it continued to harp on in a muffled sort of way, once in a while letting out a loud plea for sanity, which she treated with the contempt it deserved.

On Sunday she refused all social and family

invitations and shut herself away with one of the few
Frank Charles novels she'd never got round to reading.
A long, complex, dynastic account of turbulent times
and torrid relationships, political upheavals and
personal insights, it held her enthralled from the first
page to the last. Needless to say, her recent knowledge
of the real man behind the fantasy only increased the
power of his skill with words and ideas. She'd been
hooked on the mind and style of the writer for years; it
seemed an entirely natural development to include the
man himself in her obsession. Karl Franklyn was no
more than Frank Charles, made flesh.

There was frustration, of course, in not being able to
let him know she knew; but she could revel in her
private double-edged awareness of him, like a secret
they shared. That vivid way he had of describing people
and places and events; the delicacy, and yet honest
detail, with which he portrayed passions and emotions.
On paper, those qualities had always excited her fervent
admiration, and now she could relate them to his
personal, physical impact. The combined effect was
potent, thrilling—overwhelming; yet she had to keep it
carefully to herself.

Monday brought storms of horizontal sleet and a sky
as lowering as a heavy black cloak. Beth was afraid the
weather would put Amy off; but she should have
known better. At nine-thirty exactly, Karl's car drew up
outside the shop, decanted a slight figure clad in a shiny
raincoat, waited till the figure had reached the safe
haven inside the door, and pulled away from the kerb
before Beth had a chance even to see its driver.

Veiling her disappointment, she smiled at Amy. 'Why
don't you take that mac up to the kitchen to dry out? I
wondered if you'd make it today. Awful, isn't it?' She
shuddered, staring out at the dense rain which now
slanted across the pavements and attacked the
windows. 'Winter's arrived with a vengeance.'

'Soon be December,' Amy chortled gleefully. She
walked through to the back of the shop, holding her

dripping coat at arm's length. 'It'd take more than a bit of cold and wet to stop me coming here, Beth. You know that.' For some reason, Beth's throat constricted so that she was unable to answer for a few seconds; and before she'd found words, Amy was pausing in the doorway to add, on an intriguing note of triumphant mystery, 'Dad has something special to say to you when he calls for me tonight.' Then she vanished round the corner and up the stairs, grinning.

Beth stared after her, a faint flush rising in her cheeks, her lips slightly parted. But by the time Amy returned, ready to get on with the day, she was calmly ensconced behind her desk, going through a file of new orders. Neither of them mentioned Amy's announcement again all day, even though Beth was longing to quiz her about it and Amy was no less bursting to tell her. When it came to obstinate self-control, they were more than a match for each other.

The torrential rain and sleet had become a dull drizzle by the time Karl put in his punctual appearance at the door of the flat. He always waited until Beth had shut up shop, giving the girl and the woman time for a peaceful cup of tea together before he intruded. Then he usually joined them for one while Amy regaled him with the day's activities.

This evening he found them both waiting for him— Amy staring at him expectantly from the moment he walked in, Beth endeavouring to appear as placid and normal as possible, though inside she was seething with curiosity. 'Cup of tea?' she offered.

'Sure.' He hung his wet jacket over the back of one kitchen chair and sprawled his length on another—lean, bejeaned legs crossing at the ankles as they stretched out in front of him. Beth tried not to notice how the glow from the ceiling light created a strange halo effect as it shone through the drops of rain which clung to the coarse thickness of his hair. In one of his more expansive moods, he leaned back and grinned at them both, linking long fingers behind his damp head. 'So, what kind of a day have you two ladies had?' he drawled.

If he was aware of their tenterhooks, he wasn't letting on; and they weren't giving way and reminding him, either. 'Fine,' Amy replied eagerly. 'We did stocktaking because not many people came in today, because of the weather.' She made it sound very important and official. 'We decided what needs re-ordering, didn't we Beth?'

'We did.' Beth sipped her tea, studying Karl over the rim of her cup. He nursed his own cup, returning her gaze steadily, almost impudently. The force of his temperament was such that Beth felt her own mood rising to meet his; and quite suddenly she was seized with an urge to play with fire—to tease him a little. 'And what sort of day have *you* been having, Karl? Constructive, I hope?'

'Fine too. I got through a lot today; it's going okay.' His tone was level, but there was the light of achievement in his expression. Beth's thoughts turned wistfully to the process of writing: how wonderful it must be, to know you've come up with something really good . . . and how desperate, just as Karl's black days showed, when nothing happens, however hard you try!

'You know, Karl,' she remarked blandly, 'I've never really asked you what you do get up to, all the time Amy and I are closeted here together? She's told me you work at home, so I assume you're doing some kind of academic research over here—on a sabbatical, maybe? Or . . .' she hesitated, almost imperceptibly, 'writing?'

'Got it in two. Writing is what I do. Don't I, kid?' He turned to his daughter for verification of that simple statement; and there was just an edge of warning in his smile.

Amy was well-practised at not giving this game away, and Beth had to admire the girl's mature discretion, especially as it must be getting increasingly difficult not to drop even a clue to Beth. But her father had faith in her control, and obviously his faith was justified. 'Sure do,' she confirmed, favouring him with a brief, reassuring grin. 'He taps away all day,' she told Beth. 'It's really boring. That's why I like to come and see you,' she explained ingratiatingly.

But Beth wasn't to be put off so easily. 'What do you write?' she persisted, setting her expression into a mould of innocent interest.

He shrugged, as if dismissing the whole matter as trivial. 'Oh, sort of novels, I guess. Some short stories. I even tried a play once,' he mused vaguely.

This was an inadequate reply to say the least, and Beth pretended to be far from satisfied with it. 'What *sort* of novels?' she pressed, getting up to refill the teapot. She was enjoying the situation immensely. The two Franklyns thought they had her at a disadvantage, sharing their little joke, whereas really the last laugh was on them.

But he was quite unruffled, smiling across at her—the smile which brought small lines to the corners of those profound eyes, and caused peculiar tremors in Beth's insides. 'The usual sort,' he prevaricated. 'About people, places . . . love, hate . . .'

'Have you got into print yet? I don't think I've seen your name on any lists.' She was well under way now, determined to see how far she could push it.

'Course he has!' Amy blurted the proud claim out before stopping to think; then she subsided, slouched in her chair, glancing sideways at her father, biting her lip uncomfortably.

Neither Karl nor Beth appeared to notice her slip, however. 'One or two,' Karl acknowledged airily. 'Nothing you'd be likely to hear about. Small sales.' He waved a hand deprecatingly. 'Probably never reach this country.'

She decided it was time to accept his story. 'You mean, just Canadian publications? Only in hardback, I expect?' Hardly knowing why, she was suddenly regretting her flash of mischief. Their straightforward personal relationship was still too precarious to set at risk; his open dealings with her would surely be shattered if he realised she'd penetrated his identity as a public name. Worse, she suspected her light-hearted taunting might puncture that other commodity, so precious to any man: his dignity.

She was right: he seized gratefully on her let-out clause. 'That's it—just another impoverished author, struggling hard to make the grade into international sales, break into the paperback trade—that's me. I came over to the old country to do a bit of research and find some old-fashioned rural peace and quiet.' He leaned towards her confidingly. She had to admit he carried the whole charade off with cool panache. 'I wanted to set my next attempt in a typical English village. Where better to watch human life scurrying about its business—all those searing passions and intimate dramas tucked away under a veneer of respectability?'

That was turning the tables on her good and proper. She sat back in her seat, reeling as if from a physical shock—though the reasons for it were obscure and intangible. It was as if he'd crawled right under her own mask, just as she'd been probing under his. 'You must see much more exciting things round here than I do,' was all she said, pouring herself another cup of tea.

'And talking of village life—we have something to ask you—don't we, Amy?' Amy nodded, still clearly deciding that silence might be safer, but she turned enthusiastic blue eyes on to Beth.

'Oh yes?' In the unexpected twists of the last few minutes' conversation, Beth had forgotten all about Amy's earlier hints. Now she kept her voice nonchalant.

'Yeah. We'd like you to come over to our house and have a meal one night. Wouldn't we, Amy?'

'We sure would.' This time Amy found her tongue, appealing earnestly to Beth. 'You will, won't you Beth? Please. You've been real good to me, and I . . . we . . .' She lapsed into awkwardness, blushing as she groped

for the right words, oddly embarrassed. Then she
rallied, lifting her face to look at Beth. 'It's your turn to
eat at our house,' she said carefully, 'because—because
I've eaten at yours.'

All three of them knew just how deep that
apparently simple, superficial statement went. Beth
looked from father to daughter and then back again,
her expression calm but inwardly glowing with
pleasure at the compliment they were paying her.
Their tightly closed ranks were opening, just a little.
You didn't invite someone to your home for an
evening unless you intended to let them—if ever so
slightly—further into your private world. 'Of course I
will—I'd love to. Thank you. When would you like
me to come?'

'We thought—Friday?' Amy and Karl glanced at
each other. 'Can you come on Friday, after we finish
work here?' Amy was on the edge of her chair now,
bouncing with youthful exuberance.

Beth made a show of giving the matter serious
consideration. 'Hmm—yes, I think my diary can stand
it—I'm pretty sure I have a free hour or two on Friday.' She took off her glasses and beamed at Amy.
'I'll be there—thanks, Amy.' She turned her shining
dark eyes on to Karl. 'Thank you both for asking
me.'

'Like the girl says, it's the least we can do, to return
your hospitality.' His face was impassive, but his eyes
were warm.

'Anything I can do?' she ventured. 'I mean, can I
bring anything, or help . . .?' She schooled herself to
tread cautiously. Their domestic affairs were still a
complete blank to her; for all she knew, they might
have an army of cooks and maids. Then again, she
might have been quite wrong in her guess that there was
no lady of the house. It was all so difficult, when you
knew so much, and yet so little, about someone.

'No way.' He was adamant about that. 'When we
invite a person to our home, we look after them

properly. Just bring yourself; and make sure you're hungry.'

Before she could respond to this sardonic comment, Amy was adding: 'Dad can come and fetch you, if you like. Couldn't you, Dad?' she appealed eagerly.

'Sure, honey. If Beth wants me to.' He raised an interrogative brow at her.

'No need for that,' Beth assured them. 'Give me the address, and I'll make it under my own steam.'

He smiled and nodded. 'I kind of guessed that's what you'd say, independent lady.'

Amy frowned as she looked from her father to her new friend, intercepting some shaft of—what? Adult sympathy? or tension?—between them, which excluded her. It gave her a very peculiar feeling, and she wasn't sure whether she liked it or not. 'Funny to think,' she pointed out, deliberately drawing their attention back to her again, 'we've got to know you so well, but you don't even know where we live.'

Her words struck a chord, and Beth was still dwelling on them hours later. They'd been part of her life all of ten days—but it seemed like years. She'd noticed before how time divided into fits and starts. Long blank periods when things just chugged along in a contented haze; then sudden peaks and troughs, when acute feelings pushed themselves through to the outside, demanding to be experienced.

But was this going to be a peak or a trough? She'd been caught before, by a peak which turned out to be a trough in disguise. Then she'd sworn never to stick her neck out, only to be caught again. And here she was, doing just that.

If you didn't stick your neck out, though, how could you see what life really had to offer—what was going on around and outside your little, protected, bookish cell? It was no use withdrawing forever, hurt and stung, into a shell of literary fantasy. Eventually she was going to have to run the risk of feeling again—and now that she'd started, she had to admit it was deliciously exhilarating to give her emotions full rein once more. It was being awake, alive, alert—to pain, as well as pleasure.

Whatever was going to happen, she'd float with the tide. She was too far in to swim back now; and anyway, this current was much too strong for her to resist it.

CHAPTER FIVE

KENT, traditional hop-growing centre of England, is naturally peppered with oast-houses—those curiously slanted conical buildings where the hops are dried in kilns—though many of them have been converted into desirable rural residences these days. Strangely enough Beth had never set foot in one, either in its modernised or original state, but she knew there were several dotted around the edges of Falconden. Driving past, she often took a few seconds out to admire their tasteful transformations into comfortable homes, not to mention their ideal settings: secluded, yet surrounded by open countryside.

As soon as Karl named and described his temporary home, Beth knew exactly which one it was. Elmhurst: one of the finest conversions and locations of them all. It had originally belonged to a wealthy couple who had sold up and gone to New Zealand at least two years ago, and since then it had stood empty—presumably waiting for some other person rich enough to afford to buy and run it. And now here was that person, in the dynamic shape of Karl Franklyn, alias eminent novelist Frank Charles.

Beth couldn't resist a mild dig when he told her the address. 'Elmhurst! But that's one of the fanciest residences in the village! I thought you said,' she observed archly, 'you were an impoverished author—struggling, wasn't that the word you used? Lovely spot you've chosen for your struggle.'

She'd hardly have noticed his fleeting frown of irritation if she hadn't been watching, closely but covertly, to see how he'd react. Then he rose to the challenge as usual, smooth and confident. 'You don't think I could afford to *buy* it, surely?' He injected the

question with sceptical scorn. 'No way. We just rent it
from the estate agents. Apparently they've been looking
for a cash customer for some time,' he explained
blandly, 'but no one's come forward who can take the
place on. They said we could have the option to
purchase after a year, but . . .' he gave a short, tense
laugh, 'we're not really in that bracket.'

'But even renting it can't come exactly cheap?' Beth
was once again enjoying that illicit sensation of skating
on thin ice, probing gently as she studied him from
under her dark lashes.

'You'd be surprised.' He was prepared for that one,
too. 'It's not in very good condition, in fact it's falling
apart,' he added grimly. 'The agent isn't keen to do it
up himself, so he's letting it go at a ridiculously low
price—I think he's hoping some sucker will fall for it
and buy it anyway.'

Beth swallowed this ultra-rational explanation meekly,
and left it at that.

When she pulled her Fiat up outside in the drive at
seven o'clock on Friday, the first thing that struck her
was that Karl's protestations hadn't been entirely bluff.
Even in semi-darkness you could see the house was
beautiful, its grounds and views superb; but the whole
place was certainly crumbling. Close to, the dignified,
white-painted dwelling behind its high hedges became a
sad study in peeling walls, rotting woodwork, unkempt
gardens—and here and there, Beth noted, even a
cracked window.

But it was warm and bright inside, and Amy's
greeting was even warmer, and in her mood of slightly
anxious anticipation Beth soon forget the stab of pity
she'd felt for a proud old building, once useful and now
left to a slow decay.

Amy led her through a spacious entrance hall to an
even larger living-room: airy, perfectly-proportioned,
with its high ceiling and french window overlooking the
garden, but furnished sparsely with little more than
basic requirements. It was tasteful and comfortable

enough, Beth supposed—glancing around, instinctively searching for her host; but sombre, restrained. Spartan, that was the word. No concession to luxury, no unnecessary frills or indulgences. Here and there, small touches of colour or comfort stood out in sharp relief against the starkness of the rest: a richly glowing oriental rug, a fine painting or sculpture, a highly-polished walnut corner cabinet, plush curtains in a dense amber material. Beth recognised these instantly, intuitively, as Karl's own additions to the decor of the place. The rest, he'd obviously left just as the agent had first shown it to him.

Karl was nowhere to be seen; and Beth became aware that Amy was watching her closely, the blue eyes agitated as she waited for a reaction. 'D'you like it?'

Beth smiled at the girl. 'I think it's beautiful. You're lucky to live here, Amy. I've always thought this was a lovely house; I never expected I'd get to know anyone who actually lived here.'

'It's a bit bare,' Amy conceded, her expression relaxing at Beth's sincere praise. 'I think we should make it a bit more ... homely, but Dad says ...' she faltered to a wistful pause, and Beth encouraged her with another smile, 'as we're not staying very long, there's no point in doing anything else with it.'

'Quite.' It was difficult to keep the tremor, the shrivelling-up she felt inside, out of her tone. Faced with the prospect of Karl and Amy disappearing back to Canada, Beth was always reduced to a heap of gloom, even though she told herself over and over again that it was inevitable. Whatever they'd come to England for in the first place, they'd never made any secret of its temporary nature.

Amy was too wrapped up in her own train of thought to notice Beth's reaction. 'Anyway,' she was adding hastily, 'we couldn't afford to do major repairs, Dad says, or even small ones, so ...' she shrugged with studied nonchalance, half an eye on Beth to make sure she was getting the point.

'I should think you'd need to be pretty well off even to consider getting to grips with this place,' Beth mused, gazing round again, apparently accepting Amy's comment without question. 'But it certainly is very fine.'

A very fine house; not, perhaps, quite a home. All faded potential, wonderful raw material. Beth sighed. What a pity—what a waste of an opportunity to create the perfect environment out of ingredients which cried out to be lovingly licked into shape! Never mind—that pleasure would have to be left to some other future occupant. One could only hope the place wouldn't fall too much further into disrepair before the right person finally came along.

Amy was transparently relieved. Beth felt sorry for her, being party to this elaborate deception—especially as, if she'd but known it, there was no need in Beth's case. But there was no way round it. The time wasn't ripe for Beth to tell them she knew who Karl really was. 'I'm supposed to offer you a drink.' Amy looked important at this responsible role. 'Or would you rather see the rest of the house first?' she invited politely. But before Beth could reach a decision on that one, the youthful enthusiasm rose to the surface, overtaking the dignified poise. 'My dad's study is the best room in the house,' she confided. 'It's made out of the part where the tower is, and you can see the shape of the oast-house right over the ceiling. It's great. I could hardly believe it, when I first saw it.'

Beth managed to hide her smile of affectionate amusement at the way the young woman and the adolescent battled for the upper hand in the girl. 'I'd like to see the rest of the house,' she accepted gravely. 'Then perhaps I could have that drink afterwards?'

'Sure. Come on, then.' Amy wasted no time in taking Beth by the hand and leading her up the wide, curving staircase, prattling all the way. Beth gazed about her with growing curiosity, silently absorbing the atmosphere. Somehow, although Karl was still conspicuously absent, there was a strong sense of him imprinted on the place. He was the kind of man who left his mark wherever he went, even if he spent only a short time there. Or, Beth reflected ruefully, was it just that she was particularly susceptible to his mark, wherever he chose to leave it?

They stood in the upstairs hall—no less generous or grand than the downstairs, with its tall windows now curtained but presumably giving stunning vistas of Kent. Amy catalogued the rooms which opened off it to both sides, sometimes inviting Beth to peep in—or even to make a proper inspection, according to what room it was.

'The bathroom ... a store-room ... my dad's bedroom ... two more bedrooms ...' she pointed out each door as they came to it.

Karl's bedroom came into the peeping-in category— in the interests of modesty, Beth supposed—but she had time to register simple spare furniture and fittings; a double bed under a geometrically patterned duvet; woven rugs scattered on a parquet wood floor. It was a large, square, no-nonsense sort of room, and it was ordered and tidy—but there were a few clothes and trappings inevitably spread about, and those were of an unmistakably male nature. There wasn't a feminine, fussy touch in sight: no cosmetics on the dressing-table, no fluffy slippers by the bed, no pretty négligés hanging on the door. If Beth had needed proof of her growing theory that no Mrs Franklyn was currently in residence, this room would have provided it. Unless of course ...

'What about the other bedrooms?' she asked non-chalantly, closing the door again. 'Is one of them yours?'

'Mine's over there. You can see that last. No, these two are sort of spare. Well, one's spare, and the other one ...' She hesitated, and Beth tensed, waiting. 'Someone stays here sometimes and sleeps there,' Amy informed her curtly. 'It's only small,' she mumbled, turning away from it. 'Not worth looking at. Come and see Dad's study,' she suggested, grabbing Beth's arm before she could press the subject, and pulling her round a corner and along a short corridor.

Beth glanced back over her shoulder at the door of the mysterious bedroom where 'someone' mysteriously slept. How often was 'sometimes'? What sort of 'someone'? More to the point, what gender of 'someone'? With a real and major effort of will, she swallowed any further questions. If Amy was—as she clearly was—deeply unwilling to pursue that tack, it wasn't Beth's place to push her, or to risk any upset to the girl.

Karl's study was even finer than Amy had implied. Beth stared up into the vaulted space above the ceiling beams. 'I see what you mean about him choosing the best room in the house.' Her tone was wry, as well as impressed. 'It's amazing.'

'Well,' Amy sprang to her father's defence with endearing alacrity, 'he has to spend a lot of time in here. It's not easy, you know, writing.'

'I'm sure it isn't,' Beth soothed. 'Frustrating, too, if you don't find a market,' she mused, her eyes ranging over the smart but shabby furniture—the massive mahogany desk with the gold leather top, the bookcases lining every wall, the threadbare carpet. For an inspired best-selling author, Karl kept his working space remarkably organised. His typewriter was carefully covered, so that she couldn't even see what make it was, and surrounded with neat stacks of quarto paper. A cursory glance round would never have revealed exactly what he was writing.

The volumes on the shelves gave nothing away, either. Rows of classics—Dickens, Jane Austen, Hardy, Lawrence—alternated with more recent big names such as Doris Lessing, Norman Mailer, Anthony Burgess. With the briefest of smiles, Beth noted a few Frank Charles novels among them. So, he ranked himself in with the modern greats, without false modesty; and she warmed to him for that.

Just for a moment she closed her eyes and revelled in a secret knowledge that this was where he sat for hours on end, the latest masterpiece taking shape under his hands, fresh from that lively mind on to the keyboard. Then Amy's voice penetrated her fantasising. 'We've got thousands more books at ho . . . in Canada,' she observed airily. Something in her shrill tone suggested to Beth that she found it difficult to think of Canada as home any more. 'He could only bring a few over, of course.'

'Of course.' Beth pivoted on her heel to face the girl, hardening her private smile to a brisk, breezy one. 'It's lovely and warm, for such a tall room. In fact the whole house is nice and cosy. Must be a job to heat?'

'Yeah. Expensive too. Dad's always complaining. We have an old solid-fuel boiler, but he says if we stayed here he'd have a gas one put in.' She opened the door and stood aside so that Beth could go out first. 'We hate to be cold, Dad and I.'

Dad and I. A snug little unit, alone against the world. How long since anyone else has been part of it? Did anyone else ever intrude on it now?

Amy's own bedroom was probably the most lived-in corner of the house—pleasantly and prettily decorated and furnished, replete with posters of favourite pop-groups and film-stars on the walls, cuddly toys on the bed. Beth stood in the middle of it to look round. 'What a lovely room!'

'D'you think so? Sit down a minute. Or have a look at my books. Don't you think Robert Redford's gorgeous? Or d'you prefer Jeremy Irons? D'you like Duran Duran, or Status Quo? Or Madness? Or do you prefer Dire Straits, like my dad?'

Beth swung round, laughing, to confront this breathless barrage of teenage queries. 'No, yes, no, I don't know, and yes. In that order.'

'My dad says,' Amy continued, in terms of deep disapproval, 'there's never been anyone to touch the Rolling Stones. Or even the Who.'

'You have to make allowances for our great age,' Beth pointed out solemnly. 'I've always been a Beatles fan, myself. You can't expect us oldies to understand all the modern stuff.'

'Huh!' Amy stared gloomily at a huge poster of a punk group with spiky hair in six different colours, and safety pins stuck into a number of painful-looking places. 'Anyway,' she turned accusingly to Beth, 'you're not *that* old! You're much younger than him.'

'I'm still nearer to him than I am to you,' Beth retaliated with a grin.

Amy worked it out. 'I guess you are.' She sighed. 'Oh well.'

'You'll just have to keep working on him till he sees it your way,' Beth advised. 'By the way, where is he?' she added evenly. 'Downstairs somewhere?'

'Don't you know?' Amy looked surprised, then guilty. 'Gee, I'm sorry—I was supposed to tell you, and—and . . .' she frowned, recalling her father's precise instructions, 'present the chef's apologies, and say he'd be joining us shortly. Meanwhile I had to entertain you and show you round.'

'Which is just what you're doing.' Beth sat down on the bed. 'So, he's busy in the kitchen?' She tried to keep her tone as matter-of-fact as possible, but she was strangely overcome with fascination at the mental image of Karl turning his creative flair to cooking. 'Does he usually do it himself?'

'Sure, why not?' Amy's fair brows wrinkled, as if she considered this an odd question. 'He's real good, too. He used to do most of it, even when . . .' A faint shadow passed over the pale, pinched features. 'He always did a lot of it.' Then she sat next to Beth on the bed, becoming conspiratorial. 'Actually we have a lady who comes in to help with cleaning and everything, weekdays, and she's kinda sorry for Dad, and she likes to make things so he can heat them up in the evening. I think,' she confided, 'she's kinda struck on him, Mrs Foley.'

Beth resisted the temptation to reply that she had every sympathy with Mrs Foley's opinion of Karl.

'Your father,' she remarked blandly, instead, 'is an unusual man.'

'I know.' Amy found nothing strange in this pronouncement. 'He doesn't believe in women's place being in the kitchen, and all that stuff. He says men should be able to do anything women can do, and women should be equal to men, and he taught himself to cook and everything,' she informed Beth proudly.

For a girl to whom food was a dirty word, she was surprisingly enthusiastic about her father's culinary skills. But then again, if Karl was a keen and imaginative cook—as Beth was certain he would be—perhaps it was only to be expected if Amy deliberately chose that arena when it came to lodging her own strong protest against the crazy adult world.

Beth's musings were interrupted by a tap at the door. In an instant the subject of them dominated the doorway as if the sheer power of them had conjured him up. In his usual lean jeans, checked cotton shirtsleeves rolled up to the elbow, thumbs hooked into his belt, he surveyed the scene from beneath sardonic black brows.

'So, this is what you ladies get up to while we men slave away over hot stoves?'

'Hi Dad.' Quite unperturbed, Amy grinned happily up at him. 'I was just showing Beth the house, like you said. You did say, didn't you?' she added, a note of uncertainty edging her tone.

'Sure I did. I also said you were to offer her a drink and make her at home.' He frowned, then turned his vivid grey gaze on to Beth, where it rested.

'I did offer her one, but she said . . .' began Amy defensively; but Beth had leapt to her feet under Karl's scrutiny, suddenly tense as a coiled spring, realising for the first time that it was one thing for him to be a regular visitor to her territory, quite another to be meeting him face to face on his.

'I said I'd like to see the house first,' she assured him,

raising her eyes to his. 'Amy's been the perfect hostess, don't worry.'

He was engaged in a frank inspection of her appearance, from top to toe, and not bothering to hide his appreciation of what he saw. She'd made a special effort tonight—mainly, she'd told herself, for Amy's sake—and it showed. For Amy's sake she'd got out her favourite dress in silky dove-grey rayon, its soft folds falling over her own gentle curves from a plain round neckline, gathering lightly at slender waist and wrists. For Amy's sake she'd brushed out her hair to a rich sheen and arranged it up and back, in an almost formal style which flattered her strong facial bone structure and the smooth whiteness of her neck. For Amy's sake she'd dug out some gold drop-earrings to replace the tiny sleepers in her pierced earlobes, a plain gold bracelet which had once been her grandmother's. Perhaps for Amy's sake she'd used just a little more of her subtle flowery fragrance than she normally did; even, for a rare once in a while, worn just a touch of make-up—reserved, in Beth's book, for rather special occasions.

If Amy had noticed all the trouble her guest had gone to on her behalf, she'd hardly shown it in the excitement of welcoming Beth to her house at last. But Karl more than made up for it now. Reaching Beth in two impulsive strides, he unhooked his thumbs from his waistband, then lifted both hands to lay them very gently on her shoulders. While she was still steadying herself under the tingling impact of them, he turned her right round—all the way—slowly, firmly, his eyes sharp upon her as she moved in his grasp, trance-like.

Amy giggled, a little nervously, at the sight. 'That's it, Beth—give us a twirl.' Something was there between the two of them, something she didn't really understand—a force which made her feel angry and excited at the same time.

Neither Karl nor Beth spoke a word until she was facing him again—eyes shining, lips slightly parted—

and he dropped his hands to his sides. 'Very nice.' He took a step back. His voice was faintly husky. 'You look a picture, Beth. We should scoop you up out of your bookish den more often.'

'Beth never looks bookish!' Amy complained staunchly before Beth could answer for herself. 'She always looks nice.'

The spell broken, Karl moved over to his daughter and pulled gently at a blonde curl. 'I never said she looked bookish. I said she worked in a bookish den. You can hardly deny,' he challenged drily, 'that a bookshop is bookish. Eh, Beth?'

Still trembling from their recent contact, Beth could only shake her head and murmur, 'No.'

'There you are then.' Karl walked over to the door. When he turned to them again, his grin was playful, even boyish, but his voice carried a serious note. 'Beth knows I always think she looks just fine,' he informed them vehemently.

Once again Amy glanced at them both with a puzzled frown; then she shook her head as if they weren't worth trying to fathom. 'I was just telling Beth,' she declared, lifting her chin almost defiantly, 'that you're a great cook, Dad.'

Karl lolled against the doorframe, brows raised, hands now thrust into pockets. 'Is that right, angel face?' He shook his tangled dark head at her. 'And how would you know about that, since you so rarely deign to eat any of my efforts?'

The silence that rose between them was tangible, brittle. Amy and Beth looked everywhere but at each other. Karl looked at them both, his face expressing dry amusement. It was the first time the subject of Amy's anorexia had been openly aired in front of her, and Beth experienced a shock of anxiety, followed by irritation. So, *she* wasn't allowed to mention it to the girl—but *he* was! Well, she supposed he knew what he was doing; he was her father, after all.

Amy had nothing to say, so Beth cleared her throat,

swung her small leather bag over her shoulder and
levelled her gaze onto Karl. 'Talking of food, can I help?
And what about that drink you promised me—do I get
it, or not?'

Karl grinned. 'You get it, and you get food as well;
and no, I told you, my guests don't have to do a thing.
Just give me five minutes in the kitchen. Amy will look
after you.' Turning on his heel, he marched across the
hall and downstairs.

Back in the living-room, Amy carefully poured a small
dry sherry for Beth, a large Scotch for her father and a
measure of apple juice for herself. 'I'm not allowed
alcohol,' she grumbled, handing the schooner to Beth.
'But I like it,' she assured her, woman to woman.

'Well, maybe it wouldn't do you much good . . .' Beth
suggested tactfully.

'Especially not on a permanently empty stomach. I
know.' There was resignation in that instant retort, as if
she'd heard it all before; and perhaps a touch of
stubborn pride too? Whatever was behind the girl's
condition, Beth reflected, it was certainly complex. As if
Amy was grimly determined to keep control over her
body, to the bitter end if necessary; to prove her
autonomy, her independence of spirit, while refusing to
grow up physically into the complete woman she knew
she must ultimately become. Keeping the hostile adult
world at bay.

Beth sipped her sherry and let the subject drop. One
day, when Amy had been coming to the shop a lot
longer—when her confidence had been built up even
further—she'd broach it directly with her. But not yet.
Neither of them was ready yet.

Karl joined them a minute later, threw himself into
an ancient solid armchair and drained his whisky in
three gulps. Then he leaned back, linking his hands
behind his head in a gesture which was already heart-
wrenchingly familiar to Beth, perusing them both. 'If
you care to come through, ladies,' he drawled, 'dinner is
served.'

Tonight he was all even-tempered charm. It was impossible, as usual, not to be drawn into the potent magnetic field of his mood. Had he had a particularly good day at the typewriter? Or was it just a natural desire to set a guest at ease? There was no point in trying to work out any pattern to his volatile temperament. To Beth, it was as much part of his total fascination as his burning creativity, his alien nationality, his sheer maleness. He was light years removed from her; and yet he fitted somewhere central in her life, as if he'd been there all the time. He was a walking enigma; and yet she knew him better than she knew herself.

On the way through to the dining-room she caught a glimpse of a bright, cheerfully cluttered kitchen. Every mod. con. was in evidence, clearly in full and regular use. In the dignified dining-room, three places had been laid at one end of the long oak table, with cream linen place mats and napkins, two tall red candles in twisted matt silver holders, sparkling stemmed wineglasses, chunky Portmeirion crockery decorated with flowers and butterflies, and two enormous gold dahlia blooms in a bowl at the centre.

Beth stood for a moment behind her chair before sitting down opposite Amy, visibly stunned by this scene of polished living. 'Wow!'

Amy's eyes gleamed with pleasure at Beth's approval. 'Great, isn't it? We usually eat in the kitchen,' she admitted. 'We wanted it to be special.'

Beth wasn't sure whether or not she liked such VIP treatment. It was flattering to be feasted and fêted, and rather touching too; but in a way she'd have preferred to be simply one of the family, muck in with the way they normally did things . . .

'Right.' Karl made a dramatic entrance bearing a flaming taper with which he lit the candles. Then he blew it out and switched off the light, turning to the hatch to produce a dish of home-made pâté with wafer-thin toast. Setting it down, he sat at the head of the table between them. 'Enough of the formalities. Time to get on with the serious business of the evening.'

If this meal was anything to go by, Karl's prowess in the kitchen wasn't just a figment of Amy's filial devotion. The pâté was deliciously savoury and subtle; the chicken fricassée rich and tender, its rice light and fluffy; the salad crisp and imaginative; the coffee water-ice refreshingly different. Beth tucked into it all with her usual healthy appetite, and even Amy picked at a little of each course—though if you looked closely, she scarcely ate enough to satisfy a sparrow. But at least she was sitting there, joining in with the lively conversation, making a pretence at sharing the food. And that, Beth was astute enough to understand, didn't happen often. The realisation pleased her, in a way, more than all the rest of the meal, even the trouble Karl had taken to prepare it for her.

Amy had been allowed one small glass of cool white wine in honour of the occasion, and she sipped it slowly and solemnly, relishing the mellow fruity taste. Raising her glass, she turned to Karl and Beth, fixing each in turn with her blue eyes. 'Here's to . . .' she considered briefly, 'books!' she announced with a beam. 'Because they brought us together,' she explained.

'Books,' repeated her companions, responding gravely to this somewhat unorthodox toast, exchanging glances over the rims of their own wineglasses as they sipped.

Beth raised glowing dark eyes on to Karl's face as she set her glass down again. 'If you can write as well as you can cook,' she commented, without a flicker, 'I'm surprised you haven't made the best-seller lists by now.'

Again that pleasant shiver as she pushed at the boundaries of safety. Again he parried her advances with practised ease. 'Not all readers are as kind or gracious as you, Miss Porter.' He grinned at her. 'Maybe I should have been a professional chef instead.'

'I might be just as kind a literary critic as a

gastronomic one,' she pointed out coolly. 'You'll have to let me read some of your work, then we can see.'

He regarded her unflinchingly. 'You might, at that.'

He was so sharp, so speculative, she was consumed with an urge to back down. Searching for a new tack, she blurted out, 'My baby brother's thinking of taking up cooking for a living. He was only saying so the other day. He loves it.'

'How old's your baby brother?' Amy enquired, with deep interest.

'Nearly sixteen,' Beth informed her with a grin; and Amy's interest deepened.

'Good for him!' Karl emptied his glass and then refilled Beth's and his own. 'What you need, of course, in cooking as anything else, is a grateful public. It's been a while since I had anyone appreciative to cook for, so don't start thanking me. This was designed to be our way of thanking *you*—wasn't it, honey?' He turned to Amy.

But the girl had gone paler than ever, pushed back her barely-touched ice-cream in its metal bowl and scrambled to her feet. Tears stood at the back of the blue eyes, and her face—only just now so poised—had crumpled into misery.

Overcome with consternation, Beth half-rose too. 'Amy! What's the matter?'

Karl laid a restraining hand on her arm. 'It's okay, Beth. Don't worry,' he murmured. Then he turned to his daughter. 'Amy, you know I didn't mean anything. Come on now, don't spoil the evening,' he pleaded, low and gentle but vibrant, intense.

Shaking her head, Amy was fighting to get words out, determined not to give way completely to the violence of her sudden emotion. 'I'm sorry . . . I know you didn't mean . . . you promised you wouldn't . . .' She covered her face with her hands. Her thin shoulders heaved, but she controlled herself again. Beth could only watch in helpless sympathy: just when she'd been doing so well! 'You said you wouldn't . . .' Amy turned brimming eyes from Karl to Beth, and with a supreme effort she steadied her voice. 'I'm really sorry, Beth. I guess I must be tired. It's a bit late for me, and the wine . . . if you don't mind, I think I'll just go up to bed now.'

'Of course, love.' Beth kept her own tone as ordinary, as affectionate as she could, holding out one hand to the girl in a spontaneous gesture.

Leaning over the table, Amy took it and held it for a moment, eyes cast down. Then she dropped it and backed away as the tears threatened to break through again. 'G'night, Beth. 'Night, Dad.' She fled from the room, and Beth and Karl stared after her in silence, listening as her footsteps disappeared up the stairs. Then they turned, in one mutual movement, to stare at each other.

'What . . . why . . .?' Beth finally stuttered, bewildered by this dramatic performance.

Karl was tense and drawn himself, but totally in charge of the situation. 'It's what she's like all the time, here. It was my own stupid fault, bloody idiot that I am. I have to choose every word with such care; it's like walking over hot coals.'

'Was it the bit about the grateful public?' Beth was cautious, hesitating to speak out of turn; it was bad enough having one Franklyn deeply upset.

But he shrugged philosophically. 'Maybe—yeah, I guess she felt got at. I didn't mean it that way, of course. I was thinking of . . . I was talking about you, of course.' Surprisingly, his mouth quirked upwards at one corner—wry, even humorous. 'Don't let it get to you, Beth,' he implored. 'You see what I'm up against? Don't worry, she'll be fine—I'll go up there in a minute and sort her out. We understand each other,' he remarked ruefully. 'When it comes to jumping off the deep end, there's never been much to choose between Amy and me. That's why we're so close—too alike for comfort. And then, being on our own . . .' He faltered and paused, and his eyes strayed to a middle-distance that might have been another world. Beth waited in taut suspense: was he about to reveal more about Amy's mother?

When the silence seemed to stretch to an unbearable tension, she risked a tentative prod. 'You certainly don't *look* alike,' she observed, as dispassionately as possible.

That brought him back to earth with a bump. 'No. Well, that's just one of those things,' he replied tersely. 'Genetics. Now, how about some cheese? Or are you ready for coffee?'

She took the hint and released the subject. 'Just coffee, please, Karl. I've had more than enough to eat, and it was all wonderful. I've really enjoyed it.'

His hand crept across the table to lie on top of hers. His touch was as soft, and yet as firm, as his voice. 'We're both grateful to you for what you've done.'

She froze, then burned. Her gaze dropped, avoiding his. 'It doesn't seem I've got very far, does it?' she mumbled.

'For God's sake, Beth, don't start taking this kind of episode to heart. It happens all the time with Amy. Believe me,' he went on earnestly, 'compared to two weeks ago, Amy's like a different child.' Releasing her hand, brisk again, he stood up. 'I'll put the coffee on, then I'll go up and talk to her. I won't be more than ten minutes.' His face became a comic mask of authority. 'And I absolutely forbid you,' he commanded, 'to clear any of this stuff, or even to contemplate washing up. I have a dishwasher, and this is your evening out. Okay?'

'Okay, Karl.' She raised meek eyes to his again. 'Sure you wouldn't like me to have a word with Amy, since I'm here and it was partly my fault?'

'No, Beth. Leave it with me. Make yourself comfortable in the living-room; I'll be right with you. And,' he added, swinging round as he reached the door, 'no way was it your fault, what happened just now. If anything, it was mine.'

While he was gone, she deliberately flouted his

orders—stacking a few dishes in the hatch, rinsing glasses, putting the rest of the ice-cream in the freezer and a few other perishables in the fridge. But by the time he ran downstairs again, she was standing near the living-room window, studying a modern symbolist print on the wall, wondering what it meant and whether it was even the right way up.

She didn't move when she heard him enter; but she felt his presence as soon as it hit the room. There was a clink of cups as he set the tray down on a small table. 'Is this . . .?' she began, pointing at the painting, half-turning to speak to him.

But he was much nearer than she expected—right behind her, in fact, looking over her shoulder at the same picture. All at once they were face to face, very close. He grinned down at her. 'Paul Klee,' he explained. 'Lovely, eh?'

She did not move, or back away; in any case she wouldn't have got far, with the wall behind her. She stood still, her heart pounding but her eyes serene on his. 'How is she?' There was real concern in her voice.

'She's perfectly all right. I told you she would be, after she'd had a good cry. At one time,' he went on quietly, 'Amy wasn't even able to do that. She just held it all in. Now at least she lets it out. She'll sleep now. She's very tired.'

'She worked hard in the shop today,' Beth recalled. It seemed a long way away, the shop—a long time ago, the rest of today. 'It's been a long day for her.'

'She sent you her love. She was devastated the evening had to end that way, after it had gone so well, but she couldn't help it, Beth. She really enjoyed having you here; but I think she got a bit overwrought.'

Beth nodded, understanding only too well how the girl had felt. 'I've enjoyed it too, tell her. Please, Karl, tell her in the morning that it's quite okay, and I'll see her as soon as she feels like coming in.' She glanced at her watch: it was nine forty-five. 'Perhaps I ought to be off now, too . . . now that . . .'

'Now that our little chaperon has deserted us?' he teased, his tone light but his eyes piercing hers.

'No. Well, yes. I don't know, Karl. I've got to work tomorrow, and I . . .'

'Come now, Beth; it's early yet, for a big girl like you. I'd have been sending Amy to bed about now anyway.' He moved closer, but still he didn't touch her. 'You don't think I asked you here just for a family meal, do you?' he demanded softly.

'You didn't?' She fought down a wave of panic—or was it anticipation?

He shook his head firmly. 'I want to talk to you, Beth—in private. Just the two of us. It's high time you knew more about us, Amy and me. You've involved yourself—done so much for her—for us both,' he stressed, his voice very low, 'and you've done it on trust, and I can't let you do it any longer. It's only right you should understand why she's like she is; maybe . . .' he paused briefly, 'why I'm the way I am.'

'I see.' So, the moment of revelation was upon her at last. She was aware of a dull disappointment, and felt shocked at herself. She ought, surely, to be feeling a sharp sense of relief? But Karl's effect on her was a powerful force, and then there was the wine, and the good food, and the enclosing peace of this beautiful house . . . she pulled herself together, lifting her head to confront him with calm confidence. 'I admit I've wondered about Amy—and you—but I knew you'd tell me when you were ready, and I did promise you I wouldn't ask her . . .'

Reaching out, he took one of her hands in his. 'And you've kept that promise, I know, and it's one of the things I'm most grateful for. You're a real strong lady, Beth. Not too many people would've had the character to hold back that way.' Turning, he led her to the sofa, pulled her down beside him and swivelled to face her so that their knees touched. One of her hands was still imprisoned in both his.

The sensation of it, his skin on hers, rendered her all

but speechless. At this rate she'd hardly be able to take
in whatever he was about to tell her. Flushing from his
praise, she nodded, avoiding his gaze. 'I did wonder . . .'
she said again.

'So, it's time I enlightened you. But first,' he dropped
her hand and transferred his attention to the low coffee
table, 'we'll have a cup of this, before it gets cold. I
make excellent coffee, and I don't intend to waste it.'
He poured a cup of the strong black liquid, offered her
milk and sugar—which she refused—and handed it to
her. She sipped it, enjoying its aromatic tang, watching
as he poured his own—marvelling that those deft hands
were the very ones which translated such potent images
from his brain on to paper, for all the world to read;
that she had here, alone in her company, the very mind
from which those images stemmed.

The silence they shared was a link, not a barrier. She
knew there were acres of sympathy between them.
Acute awareness of him—the whole person that he
was—flowed through her, and all around her, wrapping
her. She was almost suffocated by it. Putting her cup
down, she steadied herself, schooled her mind to receive
what he had to say. This was no time to give way to the
huge inner need he aroused. It was a craving, a hunger;
once it took hold, she knew it would never be satisfied.

Winning her private battle, she lifted enquiring eyes
to his once more, ready to listen. But he was staring at
her, his own expression stripped bare, as raw as she'd
seen it. Wordlessly he set his own cup down beside hers.
Then he reached up to trace the outline of her cheek
and chin with one fingertip, soft as a moth, feathering it
down her neck to rest in the first folds of her dress; and
she was lost.

His gaze never leaving hers, he stretched both hands
out and lifted her glasses off her nose, and laid them on
the table beside his cup—a gentle, positive gesture, a
gesture which knew exactly where it was leading. His
hands came back to frame her face, holding it where he
wanted it to be so that he could look deep into her

warm brown eyes and read everything that must be written there; and she had no will to move or protest, or do anything except gaze back, knowing her heart was in her eyes and unable to prevent it.

She had a brief moment to register the strange conflict that filled his own eyes as they came nearer, then blurred to disturbed grey pools: there was passion there, but it was troubled; and desire, but it was muted by caution. Then she forgot everything, because she was closing her eyes and he was kissing them, one and then the other; and the hunger was swelling and spreading and taking her over, until nothing was left in the world but the gnawing pangs of it.

His lips were very soft on her eyes, tentative as they trailed down her cheek to linger at a corner of her mouth, then travelled along it in a long exploration of its curves and possibilities. Then the grip of his fingers tightened about her face as his mouth became an urgent seeker of response—not just delivering timeless messages but demanding answers to them, pressing for a way in, desperate to uncover all her most intimate secrets.

This need, this hunger, was a mutual thing. The flame which flared up between them scorched them both, equally. There was no place for coyness or pretence, and it never even occurred to Beth to hold back, because she knew she loved this man. And somehow—it seemed obvious, at the time—she always had.

She gave everything she could give, and she made demands of her own. He pressed her back, back into the cushions, and lay alongside her, his body hard and firm against hers all the way down. They were in total harmony, like expert musicians—lips, tongues, fingers playing on each other, plucking magic as if from mellow instruments. For Beth it was a revelation, a knowledge she'd waited for all her life. Whatever else had happened to her had been a childish fancy, a mere toy—a bag of sticky sherbet, sweet and full of nothing. This was the real thing; the full meal, the nourishment she'd craved ever since.

His mouth still possessing hers, he was sliding the zip of her dress, pushing it impatiently out of the way; then his hands were returning to the smoothness of her shoulders, stroking her arms, back, waist, hips, until every nerve-end was red-hot. His fingertips were sure but sensitive on her breasts, and she arched, moaning with the acute, painful joy of it—her whole body aflame with this new experience of giving itself away, yet by some mystery finding itself in the process.

Her hands followed instincts of their own, burrowing into his clothes until they discovered his body—which was broad and strong and agile and roughened with hair, and she wanted it very much, more than she'd ever wanted anything. Or anyone. It was part of him—or was he part of it? All she knew was that she wanted the whole thing, the whole man. Until this man, this body, had invaded and possessed her, she would never be whole and would always be empty. And even when he had, some primitive sense told her, this hunger for him would always return.

Lost in their world of feeling-made-flesh, neither of them heard a key being turned in a lock, a light step crossing the hallway. Knowing that once Amy was tucked up in bed she stayed there, Karl had made no attempts to secure their privacy beyond closing the living-room door.

The step approached, hesitated, seemed to listen. Then the handle turned and the intruder was on the threshold—and Karl and Beth were jerked into shocked awareness that they were not alone. For an interminable split second they both stared into blue eyes which were hard, yet almost a replica of Amy's. Then the intruder beat a hasty retreat, slamming the door behind him.

But not before they'd both, exactly in unison, gasped out his name.

'Nick!'

The single syllable echoed hollowly across the exposed spaces of the room.

CHAPTER SIX

AFTERWARDS Beth could never quite reconstruct the next few minutes. Up to that point everything had been happening fast, like a speeded-up film but with a poignant sharp clarity. From that second the film slowed to a hazy, dream-like blur.

Brutally wrenched apart, she and Karl found themselves on their feet beside the sofa—eyes searing, searching, questioning as they confronted each other, but with no word, no touch between them. Then he swung round and strode from the room, leaving her alone with her shocked thoughts and feelings.

At first she doubted the accuracy of her own vision. After all, she was both short-sighted and astigmatic; the glimpse of the intruder had been brief, the moment he'd interrupted intense; and she hadn't set eyes on Nick for over three years. Perhaps her fevered imagination had played a trick on her: dug out Nick's image from where it lurked, so near the surface and presented it to her as a painfully timely warning.

At once she dismissed that possibility as pure fancy. There was no mistaking those fair curls, or the cherubic countenance beneath them, even in that flash of an instant. Nor was there any explaining away the fact that Karl had seen them too, and put a name to them. Nick Hallett. So, he was around, just as Sal and Drew had told her; but what was he doing here at Elmhurst? What was his link with Karl and Amy Franklyn?

She crossed to the french window to push the heavy curtain aside and gaze distractedly out over the landscape. Pale silver moonlight transformed houses, fields and trees to liquid shadows and ghostly grey shapes, robbing them of all colour and substance. Yet this was surely the same familiar patch she'd known and loved all her life. Tonight everything was as strange as it was acutely real; like walking through a mirror into a world which was normal yet completely reversed.

She tensed as voices approached the door, steeling herself as it opened. The two men who entered were a study in opposites. Karl: keen-eyed, dark, rugged— almost saturnine now, the brooding frown which struck chill where she had so recently been all molten heat. Nick (and without a doubt it was Nick): as smooth and blond, limpid and bland as ever.

It was Nick who broke the brittle silence. 'Well, Beth. I heard you were back on the old scene. Good to see you again. How's life treating you?' He stood at ease, hands in the pockets of his trendy baggy-cut trousers, blue eyes calculating as they scrutinised every inch of her. Yes, the resemblance to Amy was there, sure enough, as her memory had finally realised—but what a world of spiritual difference there was between them! 'I've been wondering if we might bump into each other,' he went on laconically, when she made no reply, 'meant to look you up, but I've been dashing around . . . you know . . .'

Beth felt her hands clench into fists at her sides, and forced them open, willing herself to stay superficially cool. He might have been at a cocktail party, renewing a slight acquaintance, making meaningless small talk. But she knew him of old, well enough to read between those suave lines. He'd had no intention whatever of looking her up. In fact he'd had every intention of avoiding her like the plague. Now they were thrown together, and neither of them had any choice.

She found her voice, which was steadier than it had any right to be. She hoped her plastic smile was less stiff than it felt. 'Hallo, Nick. Yes, I did hear you were honouring us with a visit. But I didn't realise you knew . . .' Her glance moved involuntarily to Karl. Feet planted firmly apart, thumbs thrust characteristically in his belt, he watched and listened with acute intensity.

Beth tailed off, shocked at the fierce disapproval in

his face. His tone was sarcastic as he picked up her theme. 'Oh yes, we know each other pretty well, Nick and I. In fact we're all one big happy family—eh Nick?' The sardonic gaze swivelled on to the younger man.

'We certainly are.' Nick grinned, apparently quite untouched by Karl's blatant hostility. Beth recalled that she'd rarely seen him disconcerted. 'You mean to tell me Beth doesn't know?' He arched fair, symmetrical brows. 'I'd have thought Karl would've told you,' he remarked mildly to Beth, 'seeing that the two of you have become so—close.' Then he sat down, relaxed and graceful, on the arm of a chair, still smiling from one of them to the other.

'It never came up. There was no reason why it should—that I knew of.' Karl's hooded gaze met Beth's bewildered one, then dropped to his shoes. 'Nick,' he growled, 'is my brother-in-law.'

Her mouth opened and then closed again as this information filtered through her stunned brain. 'Your . . .?'

'That's right.' Nick nodded placidly, enjoying himself in the limelight of their equal amazement.

'You mean,' she ventured hopefully, 'he's married to your sister?' Even as she stared pleadingly at Karl, she was trying to remember whether he'd ever mentioned a sister.

'I don't have a sister,' Karl pointed out gruffly, as if reading her thoughts.

'No, no,' Nick explained kindly. 'You've got it the wrong way round, Beth. Karl's married to *my* sister.'

'I see.' An icy hand clenched at her heart, twisted her guts. Here at last was her missing link; and it made such excellent sense, fitted the last pieces so neatly into place. But the irony—the sheer agonising irony of it! Karl had to have had a wife—that came as no great surprise. Amy had to have a mother, somewhere. But that she should turn out to be, of all people, Nick's sister!

And who the hell was this sister, anyway? Beth rummaged through the jumble of her memories and came up with no recollection of any Hallett girls, back in the old days. There might have been a brother, a few years older than Nick—but surely she'd have remembered a sister? A female version of Nick? An original blueprint for Amy?

Clues from the past fortnight whispered round her head. How could she have been such an idiot, not to thread them logically together? *'My mother came from these parts ...'* Amy had muttered during that first conversation. Then there was Nick's sudden presence in the area, coinciding with theirs; and of course that haunting physical echo she'd noticed right from the start, without putting a label on it ...

'Young Amy,' Nick was gloating now, as if he guessed at her discomfiture and revelled in it, 'is my favourite niece.'

'Your only niece.' Karl's terse amendment was taut with cynicism.

'Now that you mention it,' Beth forced herself to observe, 'she does look quite like you.'

'Surely,' Karl shot instantly back, 'if you knew Nick as well as I gather you did, you'd have spotted the likeness straight away?' Hands on hips—wry, sceptical—he waited for her answer. Oh God, what mischief had Nick already managed to perpetrate, in those few short minutes they'd shared out in the hall?

Helpless, hopeless, Beth struggled against his irrational anger. 'She did remind me of someone, but I ... I had no reason to make any connection ... I didn't know ...' Pulling herself together, she faced up to him, lifting her chin defiantly as she gathered her resources. 'It's been three years since I saw Nick, or even heard from him. I thought he was in the States.'

'I was.' Nick yawned and stretched. 'Canada too. I get around.' He stood up, renewing his earlier inspection of Beth. 'Yes, all of three years,' he mused, 'and they've been kind to you, Beth. You're as sweet as ever—and there's something else about you, something new ...' The sly blue eyes narrowed, momentarily revealing their true nature. 'I like it. A kind of . . .' he hesitated, deliberately playing for effect, 'sensuality? Radiance?' he murmured suggestively. His tone left no room for doubt: he knew perfectly well that the soft glow which still emanated from her came direct from the intimate scene he'd just barged in on.

Goaded into action, Karl took an impetuous step in Beth's direction. Abruptly, he halted; and she felt, rather than saw, the bleak fury in his face. 'Beth.' The one rasped word seemed to accuse, beseech, threaten all at once.

Suddenly the whole situation exploded into grim farce, and she knew it was time to cut and run. The evening which had promised so much, started so well, had disintegrated into chaos. Amy had retired, hurt; Karl had failed dismally to unburden whatever he'd had on his mind. Even their mutual overflow of passion had been curtailed in embarrassment and frustration. And now Nick—harbinger of doom, raker-up of ancient stale memories—was tearing them further apart with every word he uttered.

She drew a deep breath, picked up her glasses from the table and placed them squarely on her nose. Then she found her bag where she'd left it on the floor and her jacket where she'd dropped it when she arrived, over the back of a chair. Turning at the door, she addressed the two of them in the nearest she could manage to a brisk light tone.

'I must be off. It's late, and tomorrow's my busiest day.' Her gaze rested on Karl, poised and level. 'Please tell Amy I'll be glad to see her if she can make it. And thanks for a wonderful dinner and a—a pleasant evening.' The tremor in the last three words was barely noticeable. Controlling it, she turned to Nick. 'Nice to see you again, Nick,' she lied; 'perhaps I'll see you around, now we both know where we are.'

Then she pivoted on her heel and effected a dignified exit. Neither man moved or spoke, or made any attempt to see her out. Flooded with relief, she closed the front door gently behind her and made a beeline for her little car, waiting in the wide drive between Karl's tough green Saab and a flashy white Spitfire which presumably belonged to Nick. In ten minutes, she was home.

She was about early next morning, greeting the first shoppers with her usual serenity. If they noticed the weary lines across her forehead, the sleepless smudges under her eyes, they certainly didn't say so. It was a pleasant surprise when Amy appeared at ten-thirty, apparently restored to her jaunty self.

'Hi, Beth. Say, it's a great morning. Are you busy? Sorry I'm late. Dad didn't get up, so I made them some breakfast...'

The 'them' did not escape Beth, but she restrained herself from comment, merely smiling at the girl as she carried on checking a pile of new books for a specific order. ''Morning, Amy. Yes, I'm quite busy, as you see. Would you like to go and deal with those kids over there?'

'Sure.' Amy unwound her scarf and pulled off her coat and hat, setting off towards the back of the shop to hang them up. As always Beth shook her head at the sight of that pitifully thin back view, accentuated by the tight-cut jeans.

Suddenly Amy turned, pausing a few steps away. 'We had a good evening, didn't we, Beth? You did enjoy it, didn't you?' Her eyes and tone pleaded together.

'Of course I did,' Beth assured her at once. 'Your father really can cook, and it was lovely to see where you live. I'm sorry you got a bit overtired, though. Are you sure you're okay this morning? I wondered if you'd even make it today.' It seemed odd to think that Amy's temperamental outburst had been only last night. So much else had happened since—so many new layers of feeling and discovery—it could have been another lifetime. But she must remember that as far as Amy was concerned, the evening had ended right there.

'Sure I'm okay. I'm fine.' There was relief and gratitude in the round blue eyes—as if she'd expected Beth to be offended, or annoyed, at her behaviour. 'I get that way sometimes. It's like you said—overtired, and maybe . . .' she lowered her gaze and her voice, forcing the confession out, 'I don't eat enough.'

Beth concentrated hard on her stack of books. 'If you get food like that, I can't think why,' she remarked. 'Or don't you get that standard of cuisine every day?' She was taking a small risk, she knew; but Amy couldn't be protected forever.

'Oh no. For just the two of us, Dad only makes snacks, or warms up something Mrs Foley's left. He says it's not worth cooking things specially.' For an instant, pain flitted across her features; then she grinned. 'I'm real glad you liked it, though. I hope you can come and see us a lot.' She bounced off, all beaming good humour again, the slight danger averted this time.

Throughout the morning Beth worked steadily, fending off the bewildered anxiety which had kept her awake most of the night and only increased with each hour of the day. Discovering where Nick slotted into the Franklyn jigsaw just made the whole puzzle more inscrutable than ever. She wanted details: a full explanation. Karl had been right—it was high time she was put in the picture. And now she knew about Nick she didn't want to wait any longer. The discreet patience she'd found up to now had gone up in smoke with yesterday evening's dramas. She wanted the facts, and she wanted them soon.

At one o'clock she and Amy were peacefully settled either side of her kitchen table, sharing a tin of lentil soup. Beth braced herself mentally, glanced at her companion's composed face and decided to take the plunge. Now or never, her mind advised. If Amy wasn't ready to talk about things yet, she never would be.

'I met your uncle Nick last night, after you'd gone to bed,' she announced calmly.

At once Amy stiffened visibly and put her spoon

down. 'You did? Yeah, he was there at breakfast, but I didn't know what time he came in, or if you left before he arrived, and Dad didn't say anything . . .' Wary now, she picked up the spoon again, but her precarious appetite had deserted her and she simply stirred the soup with it. 'We thought he was away for the weekend,' she explained rather feverishly. 'Last week he told us he was going on Thursday and not coming back till Monday. He was going to London to see some friends. That's why Dad . . .'

'Why Karl invited me over? Because he knew your uncle wasn't going to be there?' Beth suggested, more sharply than she'd intended.

'I guess so,' the girl muttered uncomfortably. Then she smiled at Beth. 'We wanted to have you all to ourselves. Is that so peculiar?'

Beth's tact deserted her completely in her determination to find out everything. 'But why haven't you ever said anything about him? I didn't even know you had an uncle living here, let alone that he lived with you.'

'He doesn't live with us,' contradicted Amy sulkily. 'He just stays there sometimes, when it suits him. He goes away half the time. He came over from Canada soon after we did,' she confided, waving her spoon animatedly in the air, 'and he thinks he can just use our house because we live there and he's . . . he's related . . .' There was a spirited brightness in the blue eyes now, and her voice was choked. Then she subsided. 'At least, that's what Dad says, *I* think he's okay.'

Unless Beth was much mistaken, Amy's confused reaction to her uncle was closely tied up with her feelings about her mother. It was obvious that the girl was getting upset, but for once Beth pressed on, spurred by an overwhelming need to know more. Putting her own spoon down, she leaned across the table, her eyes sharp on Amy. 'You look very like him, don't you?' she observed experimentally.

'Well, I would, wouldn't I? He's my mother's brother, isn't he?' Amy pointed out irritably.

This was the direction Beth had hoped she'd take. 'And does he look like your mother, too?' she enquired flatly.

'Oh yeah.' Amy's mouth hardened into a tight line and her eyes stared into a blank void beyond Beth's left shoulder. 'They're really alike. Not just in looks. They could be twins,' she told Beth bitterly, 'except my mother's a lot older.'

'How much older?' At last, Beth thought, she was really getting somewhere.

'I dunno ... maybe six or seven years.' Yes, that would fit in, making Nick around twenty-nine. And if his sister was so much older, it was less surprising Beth had never met her—or even heard of her. They wouldn't have been at school at the same time; and outside school, Beth's family had hardly known the Halletts at all. 'Why d'you want to know all this?' Amy demanded suddenly, her face pinched with apprehension.

At once Beth regretted her insistence in stirring up Amy's painful secrets, and her tender heart got the better of her acute curiosity—for the moment. She'd get more details direct from Karl. He'd said so himself. She must wait a bit longer. 'I'm sorry, Amy. You see, I used to know Nick, so naturally I'm quite interested ...'

But the girl was half on her feet again, pushed over that intangible edge of tolerance just as she had been last night. 'What do you mean, you *know* Uncle Nick?'

'I did once, a long time ago, but not ...' Beth cursed herself for going too far, too fast.

'But why didn't you tell me?' Amy's voice was shrill. 'All this time I was thinking you were just ... that you just liked me, for myself, but you know Uncle Nick, and that means you must have known about—everything else ...'

'No, Amy, no.' In her own vehemence Beth stood up too. 'I knew Nick—years ago. I don't know him any more. I didn't know he had anything to do with you at all. That's just a crazy coincidence. I'd never heard of you ... I never even knew he had a sister. I swear it, Amy.'

The girl's reaction was violent, and all Beth's instinct was channelled into soothing her. She gazed across the table at the gaunt face which had become so dear and so familiar, all its emotions standing out so starkly. Rage, despair, hope, in quick succession. 'You mean this whole thing is like some kind of fluke?' Amy wanted to give Beth the benefit of the doubt; but she wasn't finding it easy.

'Exactly.' Beth seized on the moment of uncertainty. 'That's exactly what it is. I wanted you for my friend because I like you a lot, and I really value your help in the shop. I promise I knew nothing about Nick being your uncle, or that he had anything to do with you at all, till last night.'

'Even though I look so like him?' Amy challenged, just as Karl had done; and Beth knew she could hardly blame either of them. How could she explain that it had been like bridging two alien worlds—different universes; having to connect two parts of herself and her life which she'd have kept separate at all costs?

'I noticed it,' she admitted quietly. 'But I put that down to—fluke, as well.'

Amy remained unconvinced, staring at Beth through wide, paranoid, startled eyes. Beth's heart lurched with guilt when she realised how she'd risked all that trust, so carefully and laboriously built up and now balanced on a knife-edge. Father and daughter were two of a kind: bruised, self-protective, deeply suspicious.

And especially suspicious when it came to Beth. Obviously their joint experience of grown women hadn't been encouraging. And who was likely to have been the most influential grown woman in both their lives? The child's mother; the man's wife.

Before she knew what she was saying, Beth had followed up this powerful train of thought with simple words. 'Amy,' it was a low, urgent appeal, straight from the heart, by-passing the mind, 'tell me about your mother. Tell me what happened, what went wrong. Please.' Then she sat down, her expectant gaze never leaving her young friend's face.

For a moment she thought Amy was going to come down on the side of maturity—follow Beth's example and find a new deposit of strength and honesty. But the moment passed, and again Beth was destined for severe disappointment. Amy scraped back her chair, clutching the table with tense, scrawny fingers, knuckles bleached. Her stare was so full of defensive hostility that it had become a fierce attack, and Beth was briefly aware of a very real fear. Speechless with irrational rage, the girl groped for words and failed to find any. Then she searched about for some other way to express her pent-up feelings. Grabbing the half-full bowl of soup, she hurled it at Beth with all her force. Instinctively Beth ducked, so that it narrowly missed her, landing with a crunch and a splat against the wall behind her chair, smashed into pieces and ended up, contents and all, on the vinyl floor below.

Having relieved the worst of her seething tension, Amy flung some muttered insults after the soup—most of them mercifully indecipherable, but Beth could just make out 'none of your damn business', and 'you're no bloody better than the rest of 'em', in there somewhere. Then she flounced from the room and down the stairs, leaving Beth too flabbergasted to move, or even call out; and seconds later the whole building reverberated to the aggressive slamming of the front door. Then there was a ringing silence.

It took a minute for the full implications of the situation to dawn on Beth. As soon as they did she was downstairs, throwing open the door, looking up and down the street. There was no sign of Amy. She ran to the corner: still no trace. She glanced at her car, then at her watch. The first eager young customers were already queuing outside the shop, waiting for their Saturday afternoon browse. There was no point in losing business just so that she could rush around after

a wayward adolescent suffering from temper tantrums—
however justifiably. Sighing, Beth turned and went
inside.

Half an hour later she'd earned herself a respite. No
one needed attention; all the children were happy in
their corner. She went back to her desk, picked up her
receiver and dialled Elmhurst. Karl's voice answered at
once.

'Karl? It's Beth.'

'Oh, hi Beth.' He sounded faintly surprised and
deeply preoccupied. She could picture him as clearly as
she could hear him: alone in that fine study, absorbed
in his creations. Nothing, but nothing, would be
allowed to get in the way of those, she supposed wryly.
'I was going to ring you later.' His tone was clipped,
laced with anxiety but no longer angry. 'I know it's
your busy time so I left it till this evening, but I did
hope we could have a talk.'

'I'm not ringing to have a talk,' she assured him
briskly. 'Listen, Karl, you mustn't worry, but . . .'

'Is something wrong?' His voice hardened. 'Beth,
what's the matter? Didn't Amy turn up this morning?
She seemed all set to go.'

'Yes, she's fine—she did turn up.' Beth kept her voice
low, one eye on the customers. 'I'm sure she's okay,
but . . .'

'What do you mean, you're sure?' Concern tightened
his tone now. 'Is she there, or not?'

'She's been here all morning, very cheerful, but we
had a bit of a . . .problem at lunchtime and she . . .'

'What kind of a problem? You mean food?' he
barked. She sighed. His temper unleashed itself as
effortlessly as his daughter's. What was it he'd said to
her, only last night, with such gentle, self-deprecating
humour? *When it comes to jumping off the deep end,
there's not much to choose between Amy and me . . .*
Could it really have been only last night? Time was
telescoping and then stretching itself out like a
slithering caterpillar.

'Just let me get a word in, Karl, and I'll tell you.' Exasperated, she glanced round the shop again. 'I can't talk now, I'm surrounded by customers, and Amy isn't here . . .'

'Not there?' he shouted. 'Then where the hell is she? Beth, what are you trying to tell me?'

'She walked out. She got upset, Karl. I ran after her but she'd gone—I couldn't see her anywhere. It was time to open the shop, so I assumed she'd go home and left her to sort herself out.' She paused, bracing herself for the inevitable explosion, but it failed to materialise so she continued. 'Hasn't she arrived home yet?'

'No, Beth. She has not.' His tone was ice-hard now. 'How long ago was this?'

'Not much more than half an hour. But I'm sure she'll be all right, Karl. It's a lovely day, and she took her coat—I checked. I expect she just needed to walk it off.'

'Walk what off?' He was grim, unnaturally restrained. She'd rather have had outright rage, she decided uneasily.

'I'm afraid I upset her. I asked a few questions. After last night . . .' She swallowed at a constriction in her throat. 'I'm sorry, Karl, but you must try and understand how I felt, finding out about Nick and everything . . .'

'Ah yes. Nick.' His tone was dry, satirical. 'And the rest of our little—charade.' She flinched. This was true anger—the controlled, harsh, bitter kind; the kind there was no shield against. 'So, I suppose you found it necessary to probe Amy on the subject of her mother? Open up the wounds we've both been so busy trying to heal? You couldn't contain yourself in patience until I told you myself?'

'I did ask her, yes.' There seemed no point in denying it, or embarking on any sort of explanation, with all these people breathing down her neck.

'So much for your promises, Beth,' he sneered. Then his voice became hoarse, shot through with despair. 'I thought you were different. I really thought I could trust you.'

'You can. Karl, you can. It was just ... please ...' An elderly man was homing in towards her, clutching a handful of paperbacks and fumbling for his wallet. 'Look, I can't talk to you now. I thought I should let you know what happened. If she doesn't turn up, will you—will you 'phone?'

'What good do you imagine that'll do?' he snapped. She held the receiver away from her ear as if it had bitten her. The man arrived at her desk and stood waiting patiently, flicking through one of his purchases. 'If this is how seriously you take your responsibilities, Beth, then it's just as well we only got as far as we did. I'd hate to trespass on your valuable time any further.'

She winced at his scathing tone; but she nodded at the man to indicate that she wouldn't be a moment. This was definitely the trickiest telephone conversation she'd ever attempted to conduct. Face to face, in the flesh, she knew she could get through this block of futile antagonism. But disembodied voices had always defeated her. 'Look, Karl.' She tried a last time—very fast, very low but very firm. 'I really am busy, or I'd have gone out to look for her myself, believe me, I would. But I do think she'll get over it and go home, and I don't think you should panic. If you're worried, you could always go and look out for her yourself,' she concluded, stung into irritation by his high-handed attitude. Responsibilities? Anyone would think she'd failed in some paid, official duty.

'I am well aware of the courses open to me, Beth, thanks.' He was arctic now, emphasising each syllable. 'And I'm grateful for your kind—advice.' He injected the word with a wealth of scorn. 'But I think maybe I should manage my own child's life from now on. Clearly it doesn't do to entrust even a part of it to *strangers*.'

The last word was spat out with such venom, he might as well have been describing hobgoblins or child-

molesters. Before she could reply, the line clicked and
buzzed, and she was left staring into an empty, lifeless
piece of plastic machinery.

Swamped with pure desolation, she replaced the
receiver. Then she blinked, gulped and faced the elderly
customer with a wan apology for a polite smile.

Amy did not turn up again that day; neither did Karl
'phone. Beth spent a miserable evening concocting all
sorts of dire emergencies in her mind but refusing to
ring and ask for a bulletin. Karl's reaction had been
nothing short of churlish. Whatever it was that had
made Amy so vulnerable, it was hardly Beth's fault. On
the contrary, she was doing all she could to help.
Anyway, nothing was likely to have hurt her in broad
daylight in a country village—was it? And there wasn't
anywhere else she could go, with no transport and little
money—was there?

Exhausted, Beth put herself to bed early, but sleep
proved predictably elusive. She heaved and twitched,
reliving those moments, barely twenty-four hours ago,
when she and Karl had shared something so close, so
deep and timeless . . . trying to equate the ardent lover
with the arrogant creature who had snarled at her down
the line this afternoon. Split personalities, that's what
people had. Heads and tails; rough and smooth;
sunshine and thunder. But why did she have to put up
with such extremes from Amy and Karl Franklyn? She
owed them nothing. They could both take their moods
and go away and . . .

No, they couldn't. She gritted her teeth and pulled her
duvet up around her. She couldn't lose them now. She
loved them—both of them. Her difficult, fierce new
friends, full of challenge and reward. Amy—already an
integral part of her life, like—like what? A daughter, or
a sister? Or somewhere between the two?

And Karl. In a lifetime's reading, Beth hadn't come
across a single word or phrase which aptly described
how she felt about Karl. There was that creative mind,

yes, and that dynamic body, both of which stirred her up out of all recognition of herself. As a whole—as a combination—what did they amount to?

They amounted to a man; a man who made her feel, with powerful clarity, her strength as a woman —and exult in it. He was a man, and she was in love with him.

Contemplating that stark fact, she finally fell asleep.

Next morning the shadows under her eyes were even more pronounced, but she made herself look as cheerfully presentable as possible for the routine Sunday lunch with her family. It would be good to see them, escape from all these complexities into their warm undemanding support. She still held out against 'phoning Karl, hoping he'd relent and contact her instead, reminding herself a dozen times that no news was good news. The machine remained stubbornly silent, however much she glared at it.

At twelve she took a final look round to make sure everything was switched off, picked up her bag and coat and set off downstairs. Reaching the entrance hall, she jumped at a sudden long, strident peal on the doorbell.

She sensed who it would be even before she opened the door; and she was right. Against all the odds, Karl dominated her doorstep—somehow taller and darker and more deeply ingrained on her consciousness than ever.

'I was just going out,' she explained unnecessarily— hoping her tone was suitably cool, but barely able to veil her surprised delight at seeing him. Whatever mood he decided to bring her—harsh anger included—his presence always seemed exactly right, a perfect fit in her life.

He cast a lazy eye over her quilted jacket, boots, knitted hat, scarf and gloves. 'Is that right?' From the three short words she could tell his fury was spent. He lifted a wry eyebrow and shoved his hands into his coat pockets. 'Looks like I only just made it in time, then.'

'In time for what?' She pushed back her sleeve,

ostentatiously consulting her watch. 'I have to be . . .'

'Cancel it.'

'Pardon?' Caught on the hop, she lost her dignity and gaped up at him.

'You heard me, Beth. I said cancel it. You're not going anywhere, except out with me.'

'But my family are expecting me,' she protested lamely.

'Give them a call,' he instructed. 'Tell them something important's cropped up. Something vital,' he stressed. The grey eyes fixed her, and she was pinned. 'We have to talk, Beth, and we have to do it right now.'

It was more like military orders than any kind of invitation. It was exciting, but it rankled; and Beth hedged. 'Amy . . .?' she began.

'Amy was back home within an hour of your 'phone call. She's absolutely fine.'

Just like that! And all night she'd been consumed with guilt and worry . . . 'You might have told me,' Beth flared, her dark eyes reproachful.

'I might,' he conceded bluntly, with a trace of that earlier arrogance. 'But I decided not to. I'm telling you now.' *I decided to let you stew a bit*, his tone implied, and she felt her temper rising to meet it.

Then she shrugged, resigned. What was the point in rekindling his irritation? He was so much less alarming without it. 'Where is she now?' She glanced behind him to where the empty Saab was parked at the kerb.

'Gone out for the day. Dear Uncle Nick—your friend and mine,' he informed her sardonically, 'has kindly invited her to spend the day visiting some friends near Bodiam. I believe they plan to look at the Castle. She seemed perfectly happy to go. I think she feels a bit sheepish,' he added. 'She sent you her apologies. Something about smashing a soup bowl?' His eyes gleamed.

She ignored his amusement. 'Didn't you want to see Bodiam Castle too? It's very fine,' she enquired coldly.

'Oh, they asked me along, but I have other things on

my mind.' He folded his arms and intensified his scrutiny of her face. 'Like taking you out to lunch.'

'Where?'

'Does it matter where, woman? We'll know that when we get there. If,' he pointed out heavily, 'we get there. Now, are you going back in there to call your parents, or do I have to do it for you?'

'You don't know their number,' she prevaricated archly.

'You'd be surprised what can be achieved with a telephone directory and a modicum of initiative,' he assured her blandly. Then he was reaching out both his hands to grasp her shoulders, gripping them in a sudden access of urgency. 'Come with me, Beth, please. If we don't see this thing through, you and I are just going to go round in circles and never get anywhere.'

She bowed her head in acknowledgment of a sharp truth. 'Come in and wait for me while I 'phone them,' she said softly.

He smiled then, closed the door and sat down on the stairs, whistling quietly through his teeth and jangling his car keys in one long, sensitive hand.

Beth walked quickly through to her shop. The wheels of her life seemed to be turning of their own accord, as if free will had totally deserted her.

CHAPTER SEVEN

BETH took little notice of Karl's remarks about knowing where they were heading when they got there. He was not the sort of man to set out on an expedition without a pretty good idea of where he'd end up. He seemed preoccupied, concentrating on the road, so she sat back and shared a companionable silence as the car purred smoothly south through the misty landscape, across the border into Sussex and down towards the coast. The day was well and truly in his hands now. She might as well give in gracefully, even enjoy being taken over for once.

As soon as he pulled up outside the rambling country inn, tucked away in a valley a few miles from Hastings, she knew he'd been doing some homework. It was a perfect place: old mellow bricks, nestling against the lower slopes of a wooded hillside; all oak beams and log fires inside—and not too many highly-polished horse brasses and copper warming pans adorning the walls. In a separate dining room, a tempting spread was laid out on a dresser: cold meats, flans and pies, home-baked rolls, cheeses, smoked fish, an unusual selection of fresh salads; and to one side, a mouth-watering display of puddings and gateaux. A blackboard announced hot dishes available from the kitchen, as well as tea and coffee. The room was filling up fast with customers, eager to sample today's offerings.

'What a lovely place!' The warmth of the atmosphere reflected itself in Beth's smile. 'I've lived round here nearly all my life and I've never heard of it. How did you manage to discover it so quickly?'

Karl was surveying the scene with an almost proprietorial satisfaction. 'Oh, I get about. I like to know what my temporary environment has up its sleeve. I talk to people, read it up, suss it out. No use living in a place unless you get the best out of it.'

There was no arguing with that. And doubtless, Beth thought, it was all useful research for the next novel—or the one after. She bent to stroke a majestic cat which snoozed, curled up on a chair by one of the fireplaces. Its fur was so long and silky, it was all but impossible to make out where its tail ended and its nose began.

'Now then.' Karl became brisk. 'Let's stake a claim over that corner over there, before someone else does.' He waved an arm towards a small secluded table, set for two, next to a window overlooking the garden. 'Then we can come back and choose what we want. Shall we crack a bottle of wine?' he invited. 'Or would you prefer something else?'

She hesitated, but only for a second. 'I'd like barley wine, please.' One of her favourite drinks, but also very potent; she had to be feeling strong and positive to order it.

'Great.' Karl grinned. 'That means I can have beer. They do a good draught bitter here, I believe.'

Beth went over to the table to leave her coat and bag as markers, while Karl disappeared to collect their drinks from the bar. Then they made the difficult choice from the array of food, and sat down with it.

'Good grief!' Beth's eyes were round as she stared at her loaded plate. 'I'll never get through this lot!'

'Sure you will. Wrap yourself on the outside of it,' he advised darkly. 'You're about to need all the sustenance you can get.' Then he picked up his knife and fork and proceeded to tuck in.

For fifteen minutes they chatted amicably as they ate, with no strain. It didn't seem to matter that each knew the other was carefully avoiding the one subject they'd come out to discuss. Beth allowed herself a brief, heady sensation of revelling in his company, without strings, while she could.

Two thirds of the way through his meat pie, Karl laid down his fork and leaned back in his chair, hands linked behind his head in that characteristic gesture. His smile was direct, without tension, reaching to the depths of those intense grey eyes—and reaching right into Beth like a laser beam. 'Okay?' The gentle, protective quality in his tone was like a caress.

'Fine thanks.' She returned the smile, but her eyes were slightly shy. 'Lovely food—thanks, Karl.'

He frowned. 'Spare me all the gratitude, for Christ's sake, Beth. I abducted you, remember? Forcibly prevented you from visiting your family? I rather doubt,' he added drily, 'whether your average hijacker gets much thanks from his victims.'

She looked down, spearing a piece of potato salad with her fork. 'I don't suppose you get away from Amy very often,' she ventured. 'With just the two of you, and not knowing many people, and her not going to school over here . . .'

'Not often,' he agreed mildly. 'Except,' he pointed out, 'when she's with you. We are all the more indebted to dear Uncle Nick,' he remarked with a glint, 'for entertaining his favourite niece today.'

'His only niece,' she corrected, meeting his eye boldly.

He grinned; then he raised his tankard to her. 'To Uncle Nick Hallett,' he announced ironically, before taking a long swig.

Beth's gaze dropped again, and she refrained from responding to his satirical toast. 'He's not the most popular person in your household, is he?'

'Oh, Amy likes him well enough, or she wouldn't have gone with him today. He can be fun—as of course you know.' His expression darkened fleetingly, his eyes sharp on her. 'But he reminds her of things she'd rather forget—or at least,' he amended heavily, 'she'd be better off forgetting. I don't have any real grudge against the man, personally—he's harmless enough, I guess. Just a bit spineless, in my opinion.' He glared at Beth as if defying her to contradict.

'Karl, I . . .' She cleared her throat. 'I want you to

know, I was involved with Nick once—three years ago . . .'

'Yes, he told me,' Karl interrupted tersely.

'But it was all over, when he—when we . . .'

'When he pushed off and left you for greener pastures?'

'There was never any future in it anyway,' she declared. 'I was naïve and stupid. All my life he'd seemed like an unattainable dream. He wasn't real; I just fell for an empty adolescent image. But at least I learned from my mistake.' She lifted her head proudly. 'No one's ever caught me that way again.' *Until now*, her mind mocked unkindly.

'He didn't seem too surprised to see you with me,' Karl commented, watching her.

'He must have heard I'd moved back here—but he can't have known I'd become friendly with you and Amy. Not unless you told him.' Her gaze was steady on his.

'I didn't,' Karl assured her bluntly. 'Moved back from where?' he demanded.

'I had a small bookshop in London when I—when it happened. I was doing well, too, till he marched into my life and tried to take it over—and me with it.' It wasn't a very flattering or dignified story; but suddenly it was vital that Karl should know exactly what Nick had done to her—and how she'd fallen for it.

He was nodding, his expression wry. 'That figures. That's the same Nick I know. Always an eye to the main chance. I don't expect you were the first, Beth, and you sure weren't the last.' His tone softened as he attempted not to wound her with inevitable home truths. 'He went on to try his luck with a whole string of women, each one lonelier than the last—and richer. Every time he got what he could from them and moved on, he was back at square one—stony broke. He never saved a bean, never got work. He just hung around us, waiting for the next pathetic sucker to come by . . .' He curbed his rising irritation, for Beth's sake.

'It's all right, Karl. You don't have to shield me. It was a long time ago, and I knew what he was really like as soon as it was finished. I had a lucky escape, really.' She managed a reassuring smile. 'I'd heard he was back—my brother and sister told me. What I didn't know was that he had any connection with you,' she told him firmly. His eyes continued to interrogate her, so she went on, gaining confidence, 'I'd noticed something about Amy—she reminded me of someone, some uncomfortable part of my past—but it took me a few days to realise . . . and then I couldn't think of any reason on earth why she should look like Nick, so I dismissed it as coincidence.'

'Some coincidence.' Karl's eyes narrowed on her face, as if he was unwilling to accept this part of her story.

She shrugged. 'Think what you like,' she said coolly. 'It's the truth.'

For a few seconds he went on studying her; then he seemed to relax. 'I guess I have to believe you, Beth. God knows I'd sooner take your word than Nick's.'

She stiffened. 'Why—what's he been saying?'

'He implied that you must have known about his link with us, and that was why you were—cultivating Amy. To get back at him—or maybe to him,' he added.

Beth felt her skin creep and redden. She struggled to control a burst of insulted indignation. She'd be more convincing if she stayed calm in the face of this accusation. 'So that's what he implied, is it? Well, I can only assure you, Karl, I had no idea he was around when I first made friends with Amy. And even when I had, I certainly didn't know he was her uncle.'

Karl continued to regard her thoughtfully; then he dropped his gaze to his plate as he resumed eating. 'My brother-in-law,' he observed.

Beth glanced quickly at him, but his face was masked. 'I never even knew he had a sister.' She hesitated, acutely aware that she was now referring to Karl's wife. Then she braced herself: it had to be said. 'I gather from Amy that she's quite a bit older than he is, and I never knew her at school, and he never said a word about her, so . . .'

'No, he wouldn't,' Karl broke in. Superficially he was poised, but a twitching muscle at his temple gave his inner tension away to Beth's concerned eyes. 'Nick's main interest in life is Nick. I'm willing to bet he hardly mentioned his family.'

Beth cast her mind painfully back to the few conversations she'd had with Nick, and found that Karl was absolutely right. Obviously he hadn't changed much since. It was depressing to think how neatly he'd pulled the rosy wool over her willing eyes. His all-consuming obsession was himself—and at the time she'd been only too glad to share it. 'No,' she acknowledged. 'Hardly at all.'

'And apart from that,' Karl pressed on, 'Caroline was by way of being the family black sheep. A skeleton in their cupboard. At that time, Nick was still their blue-eyed boy, but I don't suppose they'd have thanked him for gossiping about her.'

It was the first time he'd used his wife's name, and Beth found herself looking away, pushing the food around her plate, sipping her drink—anything to avoid facing him. But he sat silent, apparently waiting for her reaction. 'Well, if there was any gossip, it never penetrated to Falconden—or at least, not to me. I'm not a great one for listening to it, anyway,' she announced evenly. Outwardly she was cool, but secretly she was avid to know what sins Caroline Hallett had perpetrated to earn her the dubious title of Family Skeleton.

Karl wasn't fooled, however. Leaning across the table, he brought his face so close to hers that she could feel the warm breath on her skin. 'Don't kid me, Beth. You've got to be curious about Caroline? Come on now—I dragged you all the way out here to listen to a story, and this is right where it starts.' He leaned back. 'So—can you take it?'

She looked up, smiling slightly at his teasing tone. 'Of course—if you can.'

He hunched his strong shoulders. 'Sure I can. I ought to be hardened to it by now.' For the first time, she detected a note of fierce bitterness, but he quickly overcame it. 'I already told you, it's time you heard the whole sordid thing, and you sure as hell aren't going to get it from Amy, however hard you try.' She flushed, recognising a dig at her disastrous attempt to pump the girl for information. 'You'll have to settle for hearing it from me.'

She finished her salad and pushed her plate back. 'Ready when you are, Mr Franklyn.' If he could keep things light and airy, so could she.

'Okay, Miss Porter. So, picture if you will this young country girl—blonde, blue-eyed, beautiful, and utterly anarchic. Not an ounce of discipline in her. Just a bundle of repressed spirit, determined to be free of her narrow, strict, dull, middle-aged parents. Right?'

Beth nodded, her imagination fired. Even when the story was so uncomfortably close to home, the novelist in Karl took over. Her heart lurched with affection for him, the narrator so inextricably linked with the man.

'So, she reaches eighteen and leaves school, somehow picking up a few basic qualifications on the way— there's nothing wrong with her grey cells, but she suffers from a certain pathological laziness.' Beth winced. It was uncanny: he might have been describing a female version of Nick. 'Not content with the usual scenario of running off to the big city in search of thrills and fortune—as her baby brother was to do a few years later,' he added sardonically, 'she saves up her fare from family gifts and local odd jobs and then, without warning, takes off for the New World. Within weeks she disappears into the depths of America. Her parents only know she was bound for the Big Apple, but apart from a couple of postcards they never hear another word. As far as they're concerned, she's a write-off, a total disaster area. They transfer their loving attentions to young Nick, lavishing all that over-protective anxiety on him for the next six years.'

Beth was riveted. It was already making so much sense. 'What happened?'

'What happens? She makes her way gradually west to California, following the sun, working her passage—petrol pump attendant, cleaner, you know the kind of scene. Maybe the odd male sucker to help her along a bit,' he interjected tautly. 'After a year or so of this, she gets fed up and heads north, deciding to try her luck in the other Big Country.'

'Canada,' Beth murmured, half to herself.

'You're with me. At the tender age of nineteen, alone in the world—pure and unspoilt as a nymph on the outside, tough as old boots on the inside—she finds herself eking out an existence in one room of a cheap apartment house in Vancouver. Most of the other tenants are students at the University of British Columbia. One of them is a young postgraduate in the English Literature Department, busily writing his thesis and giving tutorials, getting on with his life. At twenty-two, not exactly hard or experienced in the ways of the world. In fact, as impressionable as wax, and as romantic as Lord Byron.'

It didn't take a genius to realise he was describing himself. She tried to envisage the youthful Karl Franklyn: fiery, idealistic—and unscarred by life, as the youthful Beth Porter had been before her encounter with Nick Hallett. There was a perfect, ironic symmetry about it all: that this brother and sister should have intruded on two separate lives—at different times, on opposite sides of the world—to create havoc in each. And then that the two lives should become entwined, against all the laws of probability. If Frank Charles had woven it into one of his plots, critics would have called it far-fetched. Truth was, after all, stranger than fiction.

'Do I need to spell it out?' His dark brows met in a frown. He drained the last of his beer, swallowed the last piece of his pie. 'No, I thought not,' he went on, as she shook her head. 'They saw a lot of each other. She came to his room to borrow milk, sugar, bread—then the odd coin for the meter—then the odd ten-dollar note for food. She was skint, and brave, and tough—and yet so delicate and vulnerable. He was bowled over, hypnotised—hooked, good and proper. Poor guy.' He scratched his head ruefully, as if the tragedy had all been part of some other life, nothing to do with him. 'He learned better later.'

'They got married?' Eager to hear more, Beth pushed the story forward.

But Karl was setting his own pace. 'The young man was making his way up the academic ladder. As far as anyone could tell, he was destined to be a scintillating teacher—a popular lecturer—maybe one day a brilliant professor. The girl weighed up the pros and cons—security, a safe future in a pleasant city, against shackles, loss of freedom. He was besotted enough to propose. She accepted.'

'Was she really so cold-blooded?' Beth had to ask the question. 'I mean, she must have liked him—wanted him a bit?'

'I guess she did, in her way,' he conceded flatly. 'But her way was bound up in selfishness. She couldn't even help it. It's just how she was.' He was philosophical, even stoic, but Beth read the pain and anger behind his eyes. She knew him too well, cared for him too much to be deceived. 'For a year or so, it went okay. He continued to be delighted with her, and she made a real effort to be delightful for him. Oh, there were cracks appearing in the sweet innocent façade, but he turned a blind eye to them. After all, he told himself, she had to grow up. Life had to get to her sometime. In his heart he knew really that it had got to her—long before he did.'

He paused, and she interpreted his bleak expression as self-reproach and regret. Then he smiled grimly across at her as he picked up the tale. 'She was just twenty-one when the baby was born. An angelic girl child, as fair and fine-boned as her mother. The father—a dark, earthy, unrefined sort of guy—couldn't have been more pleased.' Beth laughed openly at his view of himself—hardly flattering, though not totally inaccurate in its way. 'He adored the baby. Everything looked set for a fairy-tale happy ending.' He paused again, his eyes on an obscure distance.

'What went wrong, Karl?' she prompted softly after a few seconds.

'From that point, just about everything. First off, he discovered he was really a novelist. It was the most exciting new development of his life—but she didn't care for it one little bit. Her idea of living was getting out and about, plenty of socialising, parties, chances for her to shine and be admired. She was clever and pretty; she craved attention. The campus scene just about provided enough of all that for her, as long as her husband was a rising star within it. But when he got stuck into writing—even made a few bucks out of it . . .'

This time Beth concealed her smile. A few bucks would be a gross understatement—but this certainly wasn't the moment to pursue that piece of classified information. 'I expect she hated being stuck at home with a small baby, too?' she suggested.

His smile was wistful as he focused his eyes back on to the present, in the form of Beth's intelligent, involved face. 'Too right. The last thing Caroline needed was the responsibility of a child. Oh, Amy was no accident.' At last he gave his characters their real names and identities. 'We planned her—we both wanted a family— or so I thought. Caroline must have completely failed to work out what it would mean. After Amy was born, she just grew more and more restless and unsettled. I became absorbed in my work, and gave up most of my lecturing. I stayed at home and wrote, and looked after the baby—with a lot of help from my mother. Caroline was always out, doing her thing, mixing with people I never knew or even heard of. We drifted apart. In the end Amy was all we had in common, and even that was a tenuous link.'

Poor little girl: a classic buffer between two scarcely-communicating parents. No wonder she was unstable. 'But she didn't actually—leave?' Beth ventured.

He wagged an admonishing finger. 'You're jumping the gun, Miss Porter. How about some dessert—or coffee,' he invited disarmingly, 'to fortify us for the home stretch?'

She accepted the rebuke and the offer graciously. 'Just coffee, thanks.'

While he went over to the service hatch to order it, Beth looked about her at the other people peacefully enjoying Sunday lunch out—couples, groups, families. It was good; it felt right, to be out with Karl among a lively crowd.

He came back with two cups of black coffee, a jug of cream and a bowl of brown sugar crystals on a tray. 'Now, where was I?'

'I was jumping the gun. Caroline was unhappy. You were writing.' She stirred cream into her cup, glancing at him over the top of her glasses, which were perched on the end of her nose as usual.

'Ah yes. Well, she spent as little time with us as possible, and she attracted plenty of admirers. Moths to the flame,' he stated blankly. 'She was never without an escort, and it was mostly someone sparkling and extrovert—unlike me.'

Beth was gazing at him, frankly appalled. Again his tone was light but his eyes divulged his true feelings. 'You mean, she had affairs?'

'You could put it that way—if you wanted to be more conventional than she did.'

Beth subsided and sipped her coffee, overwhelmed with a mixture of sympathy for the man and his daughter, and a strange, angry pity for the confused young woman.

'One after the other, not to put too fine a point on it.' Karl wasn't letting himself off lightly. 'But she stayed around, basically, and I was grateful for that for Amy's sake. She was at school by now, and seemed to be a reasonably balanced kid ...' *Thanks to you*, Beth thought, but she said nothing. 'She and I got on fine—we were great pals. We lived well enough, with my books, and a bit of lecturing now and then. I sort of cut myself off ... concentrated on Amy and my work. What else could I do?' What else indeed? 'Then, about two years ago, when Amy was around twelve, Caroline's young brother hit the scene.'

'Nick.' She was wondering when he'd make an appearance. 'How did he trace her?'

'She'd kept in touch with one school friend, and the news of her reaching Vancouver and getting married eventually filtered through the system. Nick came to the States, just as she had, looking for—I don't know—the American Dream. When it failed to materialise, he came on up to Canada after his big sister—and there she was with a ready-made circle of interesting friends and a stable, roof-providing husband.' He allowed the bitterness to flow now. 'And he's been around us ever since—like a pet dog, a mascot, a hanger-on.' His despising for Nick was tangible. 'Sometimes he lived with us. Other times he went off after some harebrained, money-spinning scheme—or yet another foolish female who was temporarily dazzled by his charms. But he always came back, empty-handed. He and Caroline were fashioned from the same mould all right. As attractive as hell, but out for all they could get, and desperate for the limelight. It's just take, take all the way. Neither of them ever gave a damn thing in their life, as far as I can see.'

'Oh, Karl.' Of its own accord, it seemed, her hand crept across the table top to cover his where it lay, clenched into a fist beside his coffee cup. 'I'm sorry.'

He shook it off roughly. 'It's hardly your fault, is it?' he snapped. As she recoiled, stung, he ran the hand through his hair and sighed. 'No, I'm sorry Beth. I was doing okay up to now, but this is the bit that really hurts.'

'Would you rather not go on?' She accepted the apology willingly.

'There's no way I'm stopping now—if that's okay with you?' He glanced at his watch. 'They'll be wanting us out of here in half an hour, and I haven't got to the crunch yet.'

Knowing the crunch would explain Amy's anorexia, Beth settled back to hear him out. 'Well, as I say, things weren't good, but Nick's arrival was like a—an omen. They brought out the worst in each other, like two kids daring one another on to greater exploits. And I didn't just sit by and watch all this happen.' He straightened, glaring at Beth as if she'd accused him of lethargy. 'I raged, I cajoled, I implored. I threatened to leave. I made constructive suggestions about moving, starting a new life somewhere else, getting her a job, having another kid. I even offered to give up writing and go back to a University post. But it was too late. I couldn't get through to her. We were in separate worlds. And all the time,' he groaned, shaking his head, 'Amy went on being devoted to her mother. When Caroline was there, Amy was overjoyed. When she wasn't, Amy was miserable. It wasn't even as if Caroline ever did anything for the child. But Amy was fixated on her; not as a real, warm person, but like the fairy on the Christmas tree. Amy and I loved each other in a human, down-to-earth way, but Caroline was . . .' he groped for words, 'a fantasy figment. Larger than life.'

Beth could picture it all as vividly as if it was being enacted before her. 'Poor little Amy. And poor you.'

'Oh, I survived,' he assured her bitterly. 'I buried myself in work, and parenthood. But Amy didn't have my thick hide. When Caroline finally took off, about a year ago . . .'

'So, she did leave?' Beth pressed gently as he faltered.

'She did. She got herself a really smooth new model—young, handsome, but best of all, an actor. A member of a visiting repertory company from an eastern state. One day he'll be right there in the public eye, she reckons—and then she'll be right there with him, sharing the glamour and the worldly rewards.

That's where a man should be, in her opinion—basking in universal popularity, not lurking in a private room, a recluse behind a typewriter. Never mind if he's successful in his own field,' he added cynically—almost forgetting, in his vehemence, to guard his one well-kept secret. 'It's the spotlight Caroline needs; and I hate it. I hate hype, and publicity, and all that brash business. I just want to get on with life.'

It was a violent declaration, and it rang with sincerity. She knew it was true. No one who could write with such incisive clear-sightedness would be remotely concerned with the outer trappings of fame. He was far too sensitive. 'So, she moved on when the company left Vancouver?'

'She packed her bags, once for all, and off she went. At first I told Amy she'd be back, like she usually was. But she's no fool—she soon saw through that one. When she understood her mother really had walked out on her, she just collapsed. She freaked out. Refused to go to school, or go anywhere. Then she refused to eat. It seemed to be her only way of . . .'

'Making a mark on the crazy grown-up world?' suggested Beth at once, when he hesitated. This was familiar ground, which she'd often covered in her head.

'Exactly.' He looked at her with a new respect. 'You catch on fast, don't you, Beth? It was a weapon. It was also a way of ensuring she never had to grow up to become part of it. The doctors all said it was a classic syndrome, but they couldn't do much about it. Within weeks she was too weak to get up. She had to stay in bed all the time. Eventually she had to go into hospital, and be fed with drips and vitamin injections.' He shuddered. 'It was ghastly. The way she is now, you'd hardly know she was so bad.'

'But couldn't you have got in touch with Caroline? Told her what was happening?' It was impossible to credit such callousness, even in the woman Karl had described.

'I tried. So did Nick—to give him his due, he was as

worried about Amy as I was. We sent messages wherever we heard the company was visiting, but she never replied. Maybe she didn't stay with them. I've got no way of knowing.' He shrugged and spread his hands helplessly. 'She was so volatile—she might do anything. She obviously decided to cut herself off from us completely, just as she did from her family when she was eighteen. She never really grew up, I guess. She vanished into the big wide world to try all over again— leaving her brother as a kind of keepsake. A memento of all those lost years. With him around, we're not likely to forget her—even if we wanted to.'

'But why did you come to England?'

'Amy wasn't getting any better. I was at my wits' end, and I couldn't write—I was just looking after her all the time. Then Nick said he'd heard the company was visiting Europe, and if they did he was sure she'd come here—look up a few old friends. It was a long shot, but we were desperate. Nothing seemed to get through to Amy except the thought of seeing her mother. And after all,' he added bleakly, 'she's still my wife, and I don't give up without . . .'

Without a fight, he'd been going to say. The message was veiled, but it was there: even now, after all the anguish she'd caused, he'd have taken Caroline back. Perhaps, despite everything, he still cared for her in some deep-rooted, irrational corner of him. Steeling herself to face the thought, Beth picked up the thread he'd left dangling. 'So you dropped everything and came to Kent?'

'That's about it. Since her parents died, there's no family here, so we just took the house. Uncle Nick came along, of course,' he sneered. 'Our resident joker. I can't tell him to beat it, because we need him. The theory is, he's getting his antennae into the old network— Caroline's old mates. If we lose him, we lost our last possibility of tracking her down—if she really is over here, that is.' He sighed dejectedly. 'It's been months and there's no sign yet. Nick's not above manipulating the whole situation to suit himself, and if he wanted to visit England ... but I had to clutch at straws, and I have to admit the change of scene helped Amy at once. Just getting away from home, knowing we were seriously looking for Caroline, seems to have helped her a lot. And especially meeting you, Beth. It's made more difference than anything I tried before. She's like a new person.'

Beth glowed in the light of his generous praise. If she couldn't merit his love—if it was still booked elsewhere—at least she could earn his gratitude and respect. 'It's been great for me too, Karl, you know that,' she told him quietly. 'How long will you stay on, if there's no sign of Caroline soon?' she asked bravely.

'There's not much to keep us here—but no more to take us back to Vancouver.'

'No family—you mentioned your mother . . .?' Beth prodded gently.

'She died six years ago. My father was older—middle-aged when I was born. He died when I was twenty. I was an only child, always happy on my own. I don't go for possessions—meaningless trappings. I travel light; I carry the important things around with me, like a snail. In here.' He tapped his head. 'And Amy, of course.' He leaned back, weary and drained. His story was out at last.

Beth leaned her elbows on the table, her chin resting in her hand as she looked across at him. 'That can't have been easy, Karl. I know you like to keep your private life private. But you're right—I did need to know everything, if I'm going to go on helping Amy back to health. And I'd like to, if you'll let me,' she said simply.

Quite unexpectedly, a smile illuminated the shadows of his face. 'And what about me?' Relief from tension made his voice deep and husky.

'What about you?'

'Will you help me, too?'

Once again a quicksilver shift of mood. But she was

getting used to those, and followed it easily. 'Depends what sort of help you had in mind.'

His brows arched at that. 'Oh, I don't write scenarios in advance. I let them create themselves.' He became serious. 'You're still—interested, then, even now you know I'm an old, unhappily married man?'

'I could hardly fail to be interested in you, if I'm going to go on being involved with your daughter,' she pointed out crisply. 'I'll ignore the "old", because I don't indulge people who fish for compliments. As for your marital status,' she said carefully, 'well, I don't see see that it makes a lot of difference. Some of my best friends are married,' she remarked evasively.

He grinned and pushed his chair back. 'Cryptic lady, huh?' Then he stood up. 'You're a great listener, Beth. You're a girl in a million, you know that?' She blushed and turned away, and he shoved his hands into his pockets. 'Hey, I think we should move on. They want to clear this place, and I'm beginning to seize up. How about a stroll, to loosen up?'

A stroll was exactly what she felt like. She investigated the cloakroom while he paid the bill; then she picked up her coat and walked ahead of him, out of the cosy intimacy of the pub, into the damp freshness of the afternoon.

A short way up the road they found a Public Footpath sign and turned off down the track—across a field, along the edge of another, over a stream, round the side of a hill. Through farm gates, over stiles, following the rambling path which finally led them in a wide circle back to the same road, joining it half a mile further on. The wind was brisk, whipping colour into their faces. Karl turned the collar of his coat up among the disorder of his hair; Beth wound her scarf tighter round her neck.

There was no need for words, but when his hand reached for hers and their fingers linked, it seemed only natural. Even through two gloves the contact they made was live, sharpening everything around them.

It was after five, and dusk, when they arrived back at the shop. Karl switched off the engine and they sat wordless and motionless in the sudden cocoon of quiet. Then Beth prodded herself into action and reached for the door handle. 'Thanks for the lunch—and for the story. I didn't expect either, when I got up this morning. I'm glad to have had both.' She turned to smile as she opened the car door.

'Does it have to end here?' he demanded softly, laying a restraining hand on her arm.

'How do you mean?' As if she didn't know.

'Suppose I were to invite myself in,' he elaborated patiently, 'would you send me away with several fleas in my ear? Or would you offer me a cup of tea, in your usual kind way? Traditional British hospitality?'

She gazed through her window, away from his probing eyes. Her cheeks were flushed, her eyes sparkled—and not only from fresh air. Then she turned back. 'Who am I to refuse you a cup of tea in my humble kitchen, after the lavish lunch you've just bought me?'

He was smiling. 'No obligation, Beth. I wouldn't dream of intruding if you'd rather I didn't. After all,' he pointed out, 'I haven't been up there with you yet without Amy being around too.'

That was, it had to be admitted, a major consideration. But Beth knew when life had her by the throat. She hadn't run away from his challenge so far, and she wasn't going to now. 'No obligation, Karl. Purely voluntary on both sides. The invitation stands.'

He lifted his hand from her arm and she opened the door and got out. By the time he'd slammed his own door, locked it and marched round to join her, she was letting them both into her flat.

She led him upstairs and into the sitting room. Taking off her coat, she held out a hand automatically for Karl's—then realised he wasn't wearing it. He'd left it in the car, and come up in his old blue thick-knit sweater and jeans. She looked down at her own navy cords and matching sweatshirt. Really, you couldn't help laughing: it was like a uniform.

'Something funny?' he enquired, twitching an eyebrow at her private smirk.

'Not really.' She went into the hall to hang her coat on a hook. 'Just seeing us in our regulation dark blue gear.'

He sauntered after her, leaning in the doorway, his eyes following her every movement. 'It's this modern egalitarian society. You can't tell rich from poor, worker from thinker, east from west, male from female. Uniclass, unisex, uniform.'

'If you can't tell the difference between male and female,' she remarked, turning to go into the kitchen and put the kettle on, 'you're in a bad way.'

But he shot out a long arm, his hand grabbed her wrist, preventing her. 'We can tell the difference, can't we Beth?' He drew her towards him, ineluctably closer until she was millimetres away from him. Then he laid both hands gently on her shoulders and gazed down into her face. 'Forget the tea,' he ordered, very low. 'You and I have some unfinished business to attend to, I think.'

She made no pretence of protesting or pushing him off or backing away as he bent to brush her lips with his. The kiss was a mere tasting—hinting at earlier invasions, promising deeper ones. Her mouth opened to his like a flower to the sunlight. They clung to each other, surely two parts of the same whole.

Then, his arm round her shoulders, hers about his waist, they were walking together into her tidy bedroom, sinking together on to her neat single bed. With a mounting urgency, which fed upon itself, they were discovering one another again—passion teaching their hands speed and skill as they stripped off layers of obstructive clothing in the all-consuming need to touch the warm naked reality beneath.

They generated a new white heat which soon overtook the soaring temperatures of two nights before.

And there was that huge hunger again—the wonderful, unbearable ache of it, radiating through Beth, diffusing from the solar plexus throughout her frame and down her heavy limbs. Her mind recognised it, hazily, as desire heightened by emotion. Her body only knew that it wanted to—had to—get as close to this man as it was possible for any two human beings to be.

This time there was no untimely intrusion, nor was there any holding back. Their hands, their lips and tongues took over, intricately charting and exploring secret new territories. Flesh burned, skin melted: you could almost catch the searing scent of it.

At last Beth's craving swelled in an intolerable crescendo and she clenched her fingers among the tangle of his hair, clasping his head against her tingling breasts, arching, pleading and crying out. 'Beth!' The single word, her name, was a rumble reaching her from far away—somewhere deep in his throat. For a long instant he pulled back, raising his head to look down at her, to feast his eyes on her transfigured face. Her own eyes were shut, or she might have seen the wealth of feeling—tenderness, hardened with passion—which flooded his.

Then his mouth was upon hers again, his tautness claiming her softness, and they were no more than a double whirlwind of sensation, their minds lost to all coherent thought.

After the hurricane had reached its violent peak and shuddered itself away, they lay spent, clinging together in the wake of it. Within minutes Beth's mind was churning into action. *This time,* it intoned, *don't let me live in regret for years as a result of one instinctive episode. This time, let it be the right thing—whatever the outcome. As right as it feels at this moment.*

When her eyelids fluttered open, the first image her shining brown eyes fixed on was Karl's face, gazing down at her as if he would imprint every line, curve and hollow on his memory. When she looked at him he smiled and lifted a sensitive fingertip to outline her features, tracing the contours of her cheeks, chin, nose, eyes, and finally her mouth, where it lingered, gently parting the soft lips until she caught at it with her teeth.

'Beth.' Now the tenderness was laced with concern. 'Are you okay?'

Her heart leaped. He'd provided her anxious mind with its answer. How could it fail to be all right, this time, when his first thought was for her, rather than himself? It was like a whole new language. Its resemblance to her previous experience was, to put it mildly, superficial.

She took his head between her two hands and brought it down to hers so that she could kiss him lightly on the mouth. Then she released him and lay back, her hair spread about her on the pillow, a mature serenity dawning in her face.

'Okay?' she echoed, and pretended to give his question serious thought. Then her expression lit up into its gentle, powerful, essentially feminine smile. 'I've never felt so good in my life, Karl,' she assured him with simple honesty.

'Oh, Beth.' His voice cracked as he gathered her against him, holding her close, assuaging some of the pain and grief of those disastrous years. She knew he needed her for comfort and human warmth; to help drown his sorrow and forget his anger. And, surprisingly, she didn't care.

For a long time they lay together in their web of contented peace, while outside the sounds of a village evening gradually gave way to the sounds of a country night.

CHAPTER EIGHT

AMY'S temper appeared to have evaporated when she arrived at the shop on Monday morning. In fact she looked remarkably composed, if a little tense—and as fit as Beth had ever seen her. But Karl had been right when he suspected she was feeling sheepish. As soon as they had a few minutes to themselves she hurried over to Beth, braced herself and blurted out: 'I'm sorry about—you know—what happened Saturday.'

'Forget it, Amy.' Beth paused in her task of checking some figures to smile reassuringly.

'But your lovely bowl—and all that mess and the bad language I used at you . . .'

'It was just an old soup dish. And the mess took me all of three minutes to clear up. As for the language,' she grinned, 'I'm all for a bit of language if it helps to relieve someone's feelings. No bones or hearts broken, that's the main thing.'

Amy's expression relaxed visibly. 'Well, if you're sure—I mean, I'll pay for the damage.'

Beth laughed aloud. 'Don't be silly. It wasn't important—a tatty old bowl.' Then she became serious, studying Amy's pale contrite face. 'Actually, it's me who should be apologising.'

Amy looked surprised. 'Why? You didn't . . .'

'Oh yes I did,' Beth interrupted firmly. 'I shouldn't have asked you those personal questions. I had no right—it's your business and I certainly don't want to hurt you, and I'm very sorry.'

Amy turned away, blushing slightly, taken aback and embarrased by this generous attitude—perhaps not a thing she was used to in a grown woman. 'No, I was stupid—of course you had a right—anyhow I won't do it again. And I'm sorry I doubted your word—about

Uncle Nick, I mean—of course I believe you didn't know he was my uncle.' She drew herself up and her voice regained its normal level. 'If you ever want to know anything else you can ask me, and I promise I won't fly off the handle any more.'

Beth had her doubts about that one, but she smiled and said, 'Thanks, Amy. I appreciate that. I shouldn't need to,' she went on carefully, not sure how much Karl would have told his daughter, 'because your dad's let me in on a few more details now so I understand everything much better.'

She watched Amy for her reaction. Disarmingly, the girl grinned. 'Yeah. He said you went out together yesterday.' It was her turn to study Beth's face, still glowing with a residual radiance; and it was Beth's turn to blush. 'Did you have a good time?'

'We had a lovely lunch, and a great walk afterwards. What about you?' Beth changed the subject smoothly. 'What were Nick's friends like? Did you see the Castle?'

'Sure. It was quite interesting.' Amy managed more courtesy than conviction. 'Uncle Nick's friends were okay. They had a girl of fifteen who was nice. It's been a long time since I talked to anyone my own age—really talked,' she mused.

'Do you think you might see her again?' Beth was glad to be on safer ground. Her own new-found joy was far too secret and fragile to be shared with anyone— least of all Amy, who was in such a brittle state herself. Whatever was between Karl and Beth was too young to have a past and its future was far from certain. It existed acutely in the present, and that was where she must cherish it, hug it to herself.

Amy shrugged. 'I dunno. I guess not. They live miles away, and she goes to school and she had her own friends . . .'

'Are you beginning to miss school?' Beth wondered, cautiously. 'Now you're on the mend perhaps we should think about getting you into one round here?'

She expected this idea to be greeted with anxious

derision, but she was wrong. 'Maybe we should,' Amy agreed thoughtfully. Then she frowned. 'But then I wouldn't be able to come and help you any more.'

'That's true—but I'd have to manage, like I did before, wouldn't I? After all,' Beth pointed out, 'if you lived here you'd have to go to school, by law. Everyone under sixteen has to.'

'But we don't live here.' Beth's stomach tightened at the unwelcome reminder. 'We're only visiting. And I've been real sick. No one could make me go.'

'Of course not. And I know just how ill you've been, Amy. I was so sorry to hear about it—all of it,' she emphasised with quiet sincerity.

'Yeah well . . .' Amy shuffled her feet, eyes cast down, hands in pockets. The slight tension was broken by the arrival of two young mothers with toddlers in tow. Both women made a beeline for the romance shelves and Beth smiled over at them from her desk as Amy went off to see if she could occupy the youngsters in the children's corner for a while, giving their mothers a chance to browse in peace.

The week rushed past. Beth was too mature to allow her natural euphoria to interfere with the demands of daily routine—but it was always with her, lifting humdrum contentment into keen happiness. Even if she'd wanted to forget those shared confidences and the intense delight that had followed them, Karl was with her every evening in the flesh—a warm pulsating embodiment of her newborn feelings.

Superficially, little had changed when they were together—except that the nightly visits stretched to at least an hour while he relaxed over a pot of tea. It was almost comical how careful they both were to be normal and undemonstrative in front of Amy. Taking her cue from him, Beth kept things as low-key as possible, trying not to notice the growing sense of strain this led to. Occasionally she suspected he was regretting their brief intimacy, seeing it as weakness on his part. Her sensitive antennae, tuned to his every mood, picked up moments of withdrawal when his gaze upon her became suddenly blank, even grim. But then he would reassure her with a single potent smile, full of unspoken tender recollections and vibrant promises—and she would melt all over again into a pool of delicious physical and emotional responses.

Sunday's events were still vivid, even if they were contained in nothing but poignant glances, and she accepted his implied message: they must bide their time, for Amy's sake. They must keep those glowing embers strictly controlled, guard against giving the flames a chance to flare again. It was painfully frustrating, but she knew it was only sensible and reasonable.

At the weekend, acting on an impulse and remembering Amy's wistful comments about missing contact with her own age group, Beth tentatively invited them both to meet her family. Rather to her surprise, Karl accepted with alacrity, and Beth's parents were only too pleased to be allowed a glimpse into her usually enigmatic private life. The visit was fixed for Sunday lunch.

It was an unqualified success. Beth had explained about Amy's condition, and something of its background, knowing her parents would be the first to sympathise. Naturally she left out the full extent of her own involvement; but they knew Beth better than anyone, and it was obvious to them how deep her attachment was to this brooding man and his frail daughter. They kept their thoughts to themselves, however, simply extending their warm welcome throughout the meal and the afternoon.

Karl rewarded them by presenting his most sociable self, winning the whole family over with that unique blend of detached gravity and informed wit. For Amy it was a triumph—a revelation. Once she'd overcome an acute initial shyness, she responded to their efforts by chattering freely, even sampling a small portion of everything that was put before her. After lunch she was taken on a guided tour of the farm, growing more round-eyed with each new scene. Then she spent an hour in Lynne's room, listening to some of the latest pop music and receiving the full benefit of the older girl's worldly wisdom.

After that she permitted herself to be monopolised in a corner by Paul, who made no bones about the fact that he considered her to be about the most delectable creature he'd set eyes on all year. She sat in rapt silence, blue eyes cast demurely down under long lashes, while he regaled her with grandiose descriptions of his current and projected successes. Meeting Karl's glance as it flicked in their direction, Beth found herself sharing his spontaneous grin at the sight. This particular admiration society was certainly mutual.

While Beth joined her mother to prepare tea in the kitchen, Karl chatted to Joe in the lounge—displaying a disconcertingly profound knowledge about agriculture—and Lynne and Andrew went off to see to the milking. Val's only comment was predictably tactful. 'Amy's a lovely child isn't she—poor little thing—and isn't her father wonderful with her? So firm and yet so gentle. He's a fine man.'

'He's had to be both parents rolled into one, more or less.' Beth smiled gratefully at her mother, from whom such explicit praise was quite a rarity.

Sally, who had bounced in during this exchange, was less restrained. 'Wow! Bethy, where've you been hiding *him*? He's really something. When you've finished with him, you know where you can send him,' she announced cheekily.

'Really Sally!' Her mother's mild rebuke was automatic and affectionate.

Beth clattered some teaspoons down on to a wooden tray. 'It's not like that at all,' she proclaimed, far too vehemently. 'Don't be an idiot, Sal.'

Sally shook her pretty head and went out again, grinning knowingly. Val was looking thoughtful, pausing while she waited for the kettle to boil. 'Funny thing—little Amy reminds me of someone, but I can't think who.'

One part of the story Beth hadn't mentioned was the link with Nick, and now she stiffened. Of course her family would remember him well enough, though he'd never spent much time with them—but she'd been hoping they'd fail to make the connection. After all, she'd been far more involved with him, and it had taken her a while to see it. 'Really?' she said, concentrating on buttering toasted buns.

'Probably just a picture I've seen somewhere.' Dismissing the subject, Val passed to other matters, and Beth was only too glad to follow her lead.

But she wasn't to be let off completely. As they took their leave, amid a chorus of cheerful goodbyes, thank yous and exhortations to come again, Drew led her aside on the pretext of showing her some new lights on his van.

'Seen anything of Nick Hallett?' he demanded without preamble, his gaze direct on hers. 'I was right, wasn't I—he is around?'

'Yes, he is. I've been meaning to thank you for the timely warning, Drew.' She returned his unflinching stare. 'I've seen him once, that's all, and it helped a lot, being prepared. It was okay—you needn't have worried—but thanks,' she said again, when he seemed to be expecting her to say more.

He quirked a shrewd eyebrow. He knew his sister better than that. 'You're not telling me the whole sordid tale, are you, Lizzie? What's going on? Who are they? Go on—you can tell me,' he murmured persuasively.

'What on earth are you talking about?' she snapped irritably. It was a comfort to have the family around—but here was the reverse side of the coin, when nothing ever stayed private for very long.

'Ma and Pa could see it too, I can tell. Young Amy's the dead spit of Nick Hallett. There's got to be a link there somewhere. It can't just be coincidence.'

'If there is,' Beth stalled, taking a step back to peer through one of the van's somewhat murky windows, 'it just might not be any of our business.' With this evasive rejoinder she flashed him a fond smile and turned to walk back to the others. He stared after her retreating form, then shrugged and followed it.

When Karl pulled up outside the shop, he reached over to lay a gentle hand on top of hers as she sat beside him. It was the first time he'd openly touched her in Amy's presence, and she felt herself dissolve to a foolish, liquid helplessness. 'Coming in for a drink?' she managed to stutter, glancing at Amy over her shoulder.

But the girl was staring dreamily through the window, lost in her own contemplations. Karl grinned, tightening his grip on her hand. 'She's not with us; she's still back there at the farm with your family, and I can't say I blame her. They're great, Beth, all of them. Thanks.' His tone dropped to a low, intense pitch. 'I have a feeling this might be another miracle you've worked.'

She knew he was referring to Amy. 'You were welcome. They enjoyed it too.'

'You're so lucky, Beth.' The small voice came from the back seat. 'To come from a place like that. No wonder you're so ...' She tailed off, her immature vocabulary unable to find the right words for her adult thoughts.

There was something very touching about the comparison Amy was obviously making between her own difficult life and Beth's idyllic childhood. Beth slid her hand from under Karl's in a slight, regretful movement as she turned to smile at the girl. 'They really liked you—I know they did. They're bound to ask you over again.'

Amy's response was alive with pleasure and hope. 'You really think so? Really?'

'Definitely.' Beth nodded firmly. 'I can tell.'

'Especially Paul,' Karl teased, with the merest hint of a wink at Beth.

Amy's face, in the shadows of the car, was a study in dignified poise. 'I liked them *all*. Your parents are just so sweet, and Drew's real funny. Lynne's much less stuck-up than some of the bigger girls I know back home. Sally's pretty and always laughing. And Paul's . . .' she hesitated, unwilling to go overboard, yet desperate to talk about him, 'so clever. He's going to be a famous chef, did you know?' she informed them, with every sign of absolute confidence.

'So I understand,' Karl remarked, keeping his amusement well hidden.

'He's got to take eight O-levels first,' Beth pointed out. 'And he's quite conceited enough already. Don't you go swelling his head even more.'

'He is *not* big-headed,' came the indignant retort. Then Amy subsided crossly, knowing she'd given herself away after all.

'Well folks.' Karl's finger was on the ignition. 'Better get this young lady home. Can't sit here all night.'

'Not coming in then?' In a way, Beth was relieved. The day had been quite a strain, even though it had gone off so well. Keeping so many layers and levels of truth from so many sharp loving eyes wasn't ever easy.

'No.' He started the engine. 'Thanks, Beth, but she's tired, and if you want her assistance in the morning . . .'

'I am not tired,' came the mutter from behind them.

'Okay—well then, I've got work to do.'

Beth climbed out of the car. 'See you tomorrow.'

'See you, and thanks again.' Smiling but brisk, he slammed the door behind her. She lifted her arm to wave but the Saab was already pulling from the kerb, off into the dusk.

December blustered in with mist and sleet—and tinsel and holly in houses and shop windows. Beth had already ordered extra stocks of the kind of books that are always popular as gifts. Christmas was the busiest time of the business year, leaving her little opportunity to sit and ponder—which was probably all to the good.

Trade was so heavy that she closed the shop an hour later now; then Karl and Amy would stay on longer, sometimes sharing her light meal so that it was quite late by the time they went. Twice he brought ingredients with him and proceeded to cook them in her kitchen while she cleared up downstairs. Once, he appeared carrying a Chinese take-away for the three of them. He was friendly—but often inscrutable, always unpredictable.

Her craving to be alone with him dulled, most of the time, from a fierce pain to a nagging ache. Only late at night, when sleep hovered just out of reach, did her mind and body lay themselves bare to the longing his presence constantly triggered, yet never fulfilled. She tortured herself with empty questions. Was he simply avoiding all risk of a repeat performance? If he regretted it, was it for Amy's sake, or his own? Or even Beth's? Couldn't he have telephoned occasionally, at least, if that was the only way to have a private conversation?

Not that it would be private, of course. In the daytime, Amy was always with Beth; in the evenings, once she was finally in bed, presumably Nick was usually back. Then again, Karl liked to work late into the night, she knew that. Perhaps under her influence he was engrossed in a new book—the creative flow released again. She hoped so: that would certainly make up for a lot.

She grew uneasy, and the sharp sense of joy faded. What should she do next? Should she leave the thing to run its natural course—whatever that might be? Or could she push it along a bit; perhaps invite him over, alone, one evening? No, he'd never leave Amy on her own in the house. Nor would he willingly leave her with Nick, telling them both he was spending the time with Beth. And she could hardly drop round to Elmhurst, when she might be faced with Nick any time—the one confrontation she most dreaded, whether Karl was there or not . . .

It was a tangled web. Arguments circled round each other, never reaching any conclusion.

Then, on a Wednesday night, just as she was flinging herself into an armchair in front of the television with a cup of cocoa and some beans on toast, the telephone rang. Sighing, she heaved herself out again and went to answer it.

'Beth—is that you?' He sounded doubtful at her thin, weary greeting.

'Karl!' She found herself standing upright at the mere touch of his voice, pushing the straggling hair from her face. Then she smiled ruefully at her own reaction. As if he could actually see her! 'What's the matter? You left here only an hour ago.' She knew it didn't sound very gracious, but she was tired.

'Sorry to disturb your hard-earned peace.' There was a wry edge to his tone. 'I had to wait till Amy and Nick were both out of the way. Nick's been around rather a lot lately. They're both watching some garbage on the box now.'

'Just what I was about to do,' Beth observed drily.

'I had to catch you,' he countered, 'and I couldn't ask you in front of Amy.'

'Ask what?' She stifled a yawn of sheer exhaustion. It had been a long day.

'Come to London with me this weekend.'

'What?' She pushed her glasses on to her forehead and rubbed her eyes hard.

'Saturday, I figured—right after you close the shop— through Sunday. Maybe even Monday, if you can take a few hours off?' It was so casual, it stunned her.

'What—what for?'

'What for? Charming! A guy asks a lovely woman to spend a day or two in the great city with him—not to mention a couple of nights,' he added laconically, 'and all he gets is "what for?" What do you think? Your esteemed company of course.'

Her knuckle was white where it clenched the receiver. 'I only meant—what would we do? Where would we stay? And why now, suddenly?' Her tone hardened as the million-dollar question posed itself. 'And what about Amy?'

'Ah, Amy.' Ignoring her other queries, he chuckled.

'Poor kid—the focus of all attention and the barrier to
... real communication. The beloved spanner in the
works,' he reflected lyrically—the wordsmith in him
always uppermost. She had to smile. It was heartening
to know he'd been thinking along the same lines all this
time. 'It's okay—she's been invited to those friends of
Nick's for the weekend. The ones near Bodiam,
remember? She got on quite well with their daughter,
and she's badly in need of adolescent company—and a
break from me.'

'I see. She really wants to go?'

'Would I send her if she didn't? Especially to friends
of Nick's? Credit me with a little sensitivity, Beth.' Oh,
she did—she did. 'I'll be taking her over there Saturday
morning. We can leave any time after lunch, as soon as
you can shut up shop. So, what d'you say?'

She still prevaricated with meaningless, yet urgent
questions. 'Where would we stay?'

'No problem. Leave all that to me—my treat, of
course—no argument.'

'What would we do?' All she wanted to do was shout
yes, yes, yes; so why didn't she? What was the matter
with her, for God's sake?

'I believe there are one or two theatres, cinemas,
restaurants in London. I dare say we might just find
something to our mutual liking when it comes to killing
the long hours together,' he said with heavy irony.

She could hardly blame him. Her own reaction had
been less than ecstatic; barely even positive. She
deliberately relaxed her fingers round the receiver, and
the rest of her uncurled with them. 'I'd love to come,
Karl. Thanks for asking me.' She became efficient. 'I'll
close up at four, be ready by five. That should give us
time to get up there for the evening, whatever we decide
to do. I'm afraid I must open some of Monday, this
month, but if you can get me back at lunchtime I'll
leave opening till the afternoon.'

'That's my girl.' His delight spilled over into his tone.
'I don't have to fetch Amy till Monday night, so that

works out just fine.' His voice became deeper and more intense. 'I don't know about you, Beth, but if I don't get to see you soon—alone—I'm going to do something unfortunate to a blood vessel. I haven't forgotten . . . you understand, don't you, why I've had to play it cool? Amy likes you one hell of a lot, but she's just not ready for . . . I can't risk upsetting her.'

'Don't say any more, Karl.' Her heart sang, but she kept her tone level. 'Of course I understand. I won't say anything to her about this, of course. I'll be ready at five on Saturday. I may be in the shop, finishing a few things off, but I'll be ready. Look in there first, okay?'

'Right. I'll see you tomorrow as usual, I guess. And Beth . . .'

'Yes, Karl?'

'No . . . strings. We don't have to share a room. No pressure, you know?'

They were urgent, cryptic mutterings, but she knew exactly what he was getting at. 'I've never felt less pressurised in my life,' she assured him honestly.

There was a split-second pause; then his voice again, slightly hoarse. ''Bye, Beth.'

'Goodbye, Karl—for now.'

That night she had her first decent sleep for a week, and awakened smiling.

Saturday was a golden day—fine, crisp, clear. Even the stark bare branches struck her as intensely beautiful, silhouetted against the pale azure of the sky. You'd never think it was near the trough of the year, Beth mused as she bustled about early in the morning, preparing and packing for later. You'd never think it from her ebullient mood, either. The customers would wonder what had got into her.

The day would have dragged, but she was exceptionally busy, and there was no Amy to help. They'd be arriving now, she reflected as she snatched her quick snack at midday. Then Karl would turn the Saab round and head back to Falconden—to fetch her. Then there would be just the two of them, at last. Her pulse hammered. How she longed to be with him again—for them to get to know each other even better! It hardly mattered what they did, or where they went.

At four o'clock she firmly turfed out the remaining browsers, locked the door and pinned up a notice to say that the shop would reopen at two-thirty on Monday. Then she raced upstairs to get ready. Her case was packed. All she had to do was wash and change into the dress she'd chosen that morning—her most recent purchase, a bib-front pinafore in brown and fawn checks, with a wide skirt and deep seam pockets, which she wore with a coffee-coloured silk blouse. Then she pulled on her knee-length leather boots, brushed out her shining hair, applied a little discreet make-up and surveyed herself in the long mirror. As an afterthought she donned a smart russet-brown beret, matching her coat and scarf, tilted at a jaunty angle to one side of her head. She didn't often wear it, but it seemed to suit her mood today.

With a last look round the flat, she set off downstairs. It was four-thirty—plenty of time to tidy up a few ends before she could leave the shop unattended for two nights. Two nights! Heaven knew how she'd be feeling when she got home on Monday—but she certainly had no intention of walking back into anything less than perfect order here.

She hummed as she straightened books on shelves, sorted out cash from cheques, locked the day's takings away, cleared surfaces, closed drawers and finally ran a hoover over the carpet. Outside, darkness had fallen in its depressingly early midwinter way—gloomy, and yet rather cosy when one was indoors in a bright warm atmosphere. Seasonal fairy-lights twinkled in neighbouring shops. It was going to be cold, it was so clear—and there'd be a glorious powdering of stars soon against that velvet blackness. Then the glittering lights of London, with all they represented! She shivered with excited anticipation.

As she carried a pile of books through to the stockroom, she was arrested in her tracks by a tapping at the glass door of the shop. Balancing the top book under her chin, she pulled up her sleeve to consult her watch. Four-forty: he was early. Never mind—he could come in anyway, wait a few minutes while she saw to the final touches. Then they could go.

It was too dark to make out the figure waiting in the shadows until she'd opened the door and stood, smiling her warm welcome, floodlit in the neon glare from the shop. When she did make him out, the wide smile rapidly disappeared. She had no smiles for this man. This was the wrong man, in every possible sense.

'Nick—what are you doing here?' Panic flooded her, numbing her brain, tensing her body. 'Is anything wrong?' Surely he didn't bring bad news—a message . . .?

'Does something have to be wrong, just because I come to see you?' he drawled in his newly-acquired midatlantic accent, holding out his hands in a theatrical gesture. 'Closed already?' He stared behind her into the shop, then directly into her face and down her body—registering her high colour and smart appearance. 'Going out?'

He took a pace towards her and she stepped back instinctively, letting go of the door. Seizing his chance he walked past her across the threshold, pushing the door shut as he went. His hard blue eyes shot curious darts, taking in every detail of the place—its air of confident success, its attractive displays and well-maintained decor. Beth froze briefly. Nick's arrival at this moment was a potential disaster.

Then she rallied, steadying herself to cope. 'Yes, I'm going out. As I rather suspect you knew.'

His pout was all injured innocence. 'How would I know a thing like that? What do I know about your . . .' he leered, 'private life, these days?'

One look at the curl of that perfectly-shaped upper lip confirmed her suspicions. He knew full well what was going on. No doubt he'd picked up some of their 'phone call on Wednesday. She saw red, literally, at this insight into how infuriating, how impossible Karl's life must be with Nick always on the fringes of it. But she forced herself to see this crisis through rationally, for all their sakes.

'Nick, it's nice to see you but I can't talk now. I'm off in a few minutes. That's why I closed early. Could you come back one day next week?'

His eyes widened. ' *"Nice to see me"?*' he echoed, mimicking her wooden tone. 'Whatever would my dear brother-in-law think about that? All this time you've kept scrupulously out of the way—I might be the ghost of Hamlet's father to judge by my popularity ratings around here. Now I finally come to check you out for myself, and you invite me to come back? What's your game, Beth?'

There was menace in his mockery, and Beth was gripped by a cold sense of foreboding. Nick had never wished her well, and he did not wish her well now. Giving up the pretence of amicability, she confronted him with her real hostility. 'What did you come here for, Nick? What do you want?'

'That's better,' he said comfortably. 'Now we know where we stand.' His eyes were still busily appraising her. 'I must say, little Beth, you know how to get yourself up, these days. You've ripened beautifully. I'm honoured,' he made a small satirical bow, 'to have been offered first bite of such a luscious peach. Or is it highly ungentlemanly and indelicate of me to say so?' His eyes gleamed with malicious enjoyment, but his face was as bland as ever.

'You can say anything you like—another time,' she replied coolly. 'Now I just want you to leave. In ten minutes I have to be out of here.' And Karl would be here, her mind added darkly. She moved towards the door, ready to open it for him, struggling to mask her growing desperation.

'Come now, Beth—surely there's no need to be quite

so melodramatic?' His manner was still suave, but his eyes had narrowed. 'Or have you got a train to catch?'

Her own eyes flickered across his features. Did he know she was going out with Karl—or not? He'd always been so good at giving nothing away. Probably he did; but she must play it cool just in case he didn't. 'I'm not being dramatic. I just want to get ready and go, that's all. If you want to see me, you could have dropped by any time,' she argued reasonably.

'I could, could I? And could I have been sure of a welcome on the mat, like Karl and Amy?' His mask was almost slipping, but he retrieved it. 'Well, perhaps I haven't been interested enough—till now.' He came further into the shop, ignoring the arm she held out to prevent him. Nochalantly he surveyed the scene again. 'Pleasant place you've built up here, Beth. Big, too. Doing well, is it?'

His tone rose as he phrased the question. All at once she found she pitied him. Despite everything, he was still on the make. What was it Karl had said—*an eye to the main chance.* Yes, that was Nick. He was pathetic really. It made her feel sick to think she had ever liked him—wanted him—cared for him at all.

'I do all right, thanks.'

'Why did you sell up the London shop? I'd have thought the future was better there?' he enquired, apparently casual.

As if he didn't know! She regarded him thoughtfully; perhaps he really didn't know? 'I decided,' she told him evenly, 'it was time to come back to the country.'

His expression moulded itself into remorse. He knew, all right. Nick was no more than a consummate play-actor—an art he'd been polishing further these past years. All outer show, no inner strength—a bright empty shell, just like his sister. Yes, pity was the operative emotion. He wasn't worth hating. Pity; as well as a profound determination to stop him using Karl, or influencing Amy, any more than he already had. 'It wasn't all because of me, was it, Beth?'

He moved closer to her, holding out one hand as a sign of appeasement. She stayed where she was. 'Good lord, no. Whatever gave you that idea?' Two could play at his game, even if acting didn't come so naturally to her. 'I knew as well as you did that our—affair was a temporary thing.' Her stumble over the word was barely perceptible. 'When you moved on it was much the best thing for us both. In fact,' she added tautly, 'you did me a favour.'

'You don't think I might have made a mistake?' His voice was soft, insinuating.

She tightened all over. 'A mistake? I should imagine you've made plenty.' Her tone wavered dangerously with suppressed scorn and dislike.

'About leaving you, I mean.' He came even closer; still she stood her ground. 'Any chance of giving it another try, Beth? We're older and wiser now. I've often thought about you since. I'm sure we'd have more to offer each other this time.'

'You mean I'd have an even bigger, better business to offer you.' Cold rage solidified her face so that she could scarcely force the words out. 'Oh, it would suit you just perfectly, wouldn't it, Nick? Not just a second bite out of the even riper, richer peach . . .' Her hands clenched into fists at her sides. 'A chance to get at Karl too. Magic!'

His hands came up then, to grip her arms; but his voice was pure honey. 'Such a lovely lady with such a mean streak!' he lamented. 'You never used to be so tough, Miss Porter—one would never guess it to look at you—such a nasty suspicious nature. Brother Karl must have been really busy indoctrinating you against me—and my poor sister. His wife,' he reminded her unpleasantly. 'You shouldn't believe everything you hear,' he added lightly, 'from a professional story-teller.'

'*He is not your brother!*' The very idea was nauseating. It was bad enough that he was Amy's blood relative, without being accused of being Karl's too.

Nick's grip tightened, but his face remained bland and his voice mellifluous. 'Pardon the insult, I'm sure. Just a manner of speaking. You know who he is, of course—professionally, that is?' There was wickedness in the query, a deliberate attempt to stir up trouble between them.

'As it happens,' she retorted, 'I do. I've known all along about his pen-name.'

The fair brows formed a perfect arch. 'The hell you did? I must say, you surprise me. The great Frank Charles usually guards his true identity as closely as he protects his beloved offspring's interests.' He brought his face closer to hers. 'So, being in the trade, you'll be aware that he's one of the world's top sellers. Not the unknown recluse, nor the penniless author, he likes to pretend to be.'

'He deserves every bit of his success,' Beth declared hotly. 'He's one of the best writers around at the moment.'

'Got it bad, eh?' he murmured. He was far too close. Revulsion swamped her, but she refused to struggle, however much her body wanted to. She knew that would only inflame his obscure desires. If she stayed cold and unmoved, surely he'd give up and go away? Time was running out; she had to get rid of him.

'You can't get at me through Karl,' she told him steadily. 'And you won't get at Karl through me. So why don't you just get out of here? You won't achieve anything by—all this.' Her voice rose, gathering momentum. 'Anything between you and me was just fantasy—you know that as well as I do. I was young and stupid, you were out for what you could get—and you still are.' She abandoned the fight to control her seething bitterness. 'Why don't you run along and find another poor sad rich female to leech on to? At least your sister had the integrity to cut out and follow her own path—not to hang about waiting for subsidies— for the fruits of someone else's labours to fall off the tree. Even if she did ruin a man's life, and a child's, at least she gave up when she'd done enough damage. You know she'll never be back, and what's more, I don't believe you've got the slightest idea where she is. You never really expected her to come back here, after so many years, did you Nick? You just fancied a trip home, and you knew Karl would try anything to help Amy. You're just cashing in cynically on his natural concern for her.'

Reaching the climax of her tirade, she paused to draw breath before flinging the final accusation. 'You don't give a toss for either of them. All you've ever cared about is yourself.' Eyes flashing, she stood, awaiting his reaction.

It was never Nick's way to counter anger with anger. He became defensive, petulant—shrinking like a chastened child. She knew she'd hit a deep target. 'What do you know about my sister?' he mumbled sullenly. 'I never even mentioned her to you—till the other night. I suppose Karl wasted no time putting you in the picture?'

'And when he did,' she returned, 'I understood a lot more about you, as well as him.'

She was still glaring up at him, her face set into a harsh mask of stored rage. Suddenly, without warning, his crumpled. It was like looking at a plastic doll melting in searing heat. It was the most extraordinary image she'd ever seen. Mesmerised, she watched as lines and sags and hollows creased the smooth features, transforming them into a real, suffering travesty of his public self. A portrait of Dorian Gray, her literary mind suggested, even as she gazed at it.

The honey drained from his voice, leaving a rasping, torn croak. 'Beth, I—I want to find her, as much as they do. If she's not with them, then I've got no place with them. And if I can't stay with them, what can I do? I'm no good at anything. All I've ever been any good at is ... being beautiful. In the end, who wants you for that? You get older. You don't even stay beautiful.'

His despair and self-loathing were tangible.

Astonished, she stared up into the working, struggling face. Of all the effects her indignant outburst might have had, this was the last she'd expected. 'Of course you could do something else,' she snorted. 'Don't be such a weak, self-indulgent fool.'

'That's just it,' he moaned. 'I'm the fool, the joker in the pack, the court jester. Karl used to tolerate me for Caro's sake—he knew she liked me being around. Then for Amy's sake, because I remind her of her mother. He knows I'm fond of the kid in my way, and she quite likes me.' He rallied for one last dig at her. 'Karl adored Caro, Beth. If you could have seen him when she finally left . . .'

Then he was breaking down completely, gathering her soft body to him, blindly seeking comfort from contact with another human being. There was nothing sexual about it; he was like a child. She could feel tears on her temple, where his eyes brushed against it as he burrowed his collapsed face into the warmth of her neck.

She stood patiently, neither responding nor rejecting, while he sobbed out his pent-up miseries. There was nothing else she could do. Shock obliterated everything else for a minute—even thoughts of Karl and the weekend ahead. The bright shop lights shone down on the tableau they presented—man and woman, apparently frozen into an infinite, archetypal embrace. Outside the shadows deepened and early stars began to pinpoint their complex patterns on the sky.

The big green car drew smoothly to a halt; the powerful energetic figure crossed the pavement to the shop door. He peered inside, knuckles raised ready to knock. Then he halted, hesitated, gazed in for a long moment—and turned decisively away.

By the time Beth had disentangled herself from Nick's shaking form, pushed him off and sprung to the door, Karl had leaped back into the driving seat and roared away. Nothing was left but a small cloud of exhaust fumes hanging in the frosty air.

CHAPTER NINE

ONE look at her face, contorted with speechless rage—and her body, trembling violently from head to foot—and Nick bolted like a terrified animal. Out into the night, slamming the door of his Spitfire (parked carefully out of sight round a corner), accelerating away from the damage he knew he had caused—evading his responsibility just as he always had done, always would do.

Beth's head contained not one single coherent thought; just a dark red murderous streak. If he crashed his car and died in agony, it would serve him right. If she never saw him again it would be too soon.

As it happened, it was to be many years before she did; and by that time these poignant events existed in another dimension, like peering through the wrong end of a telescope—vaguely perceiving your own past down a long hazy tunnel.

When reason took over, she was still paper-white and shaking—and cold. Nick had left the door swinging open. She crossed slowly over to close it, first gazing distractedly up and down the street. It was early yet, and people hurried by, cars swooped past. But of course there was no sign of Karl.

He'd come to her, keyed up—as she was—for their crucial, climactic weekend together. He'd confronted a scene which seemed to give the lie to every one of her earnest protestations about Nick's place in her life. And he'd turned straight round and gone away again. Beth knew him well enough to understand why. If he'd come in and faced them, there'd have been no accounting for the ferocity of his actions or reactions. He'd almost certainly have hit Nick right where it hurt—and quite possibly Beth too.

Sick and faint, she wrapped limp arms about her shuddering body as she stumbled upstairs. There, she sat among the order of her flat, not even bothering to switch on any lights. Perhaps he'd be back, once he'd thought it all through?

Gradually the shock wore off and she stiffened herself for action. It was no use sitting around like a zombie. The vital thing was to reach Karl, this time, before Nick himself could—before he could achieve yet more irreparable damage between them. In his volatile, bruised state, Karl might believe anything. It was her word against Nick's, and Nick would go to any length in the world to get himself out of a jam—especially when it came to losing favour with Karl. He was totally unscrupulous.

Mouth dry, heart racing, she forced herself to the telephone and dialled Elmhurst. The ringing tone went on and on, with that hollow, mocking resonance which always seems to denote an empty house. Wherever he was, he wasn't there. No point in leaping into her car and following him, either; he might be anywhere. Headed for London without her. Driving furiously through the countryside, putting himself and others at risk . . . it didn't bear thinking about. She crashed the receiver back into its cradle. There was nothing to do but wait.

Far into the evening, sitting in the dark, she waited. Three times—or was it four, five?—she tried the number again. No reply. Neither man had returned home—or if they had, they weren't answering. Should she go round there? But what if Karl wasn't there, and Nick was? No way could she risk that. She stayed.

Eventually, with the first cold fingers of dawn, she drifted into a fitful doze. At nine o'clock she jerked into life—slumped, hunched, twisted in her armchair. Her whole body felt racked, tense, chilled—but that was nothing compared with the gnawing ache of loss beneath. Such a build-up, such a crashing-down!

She sipped a cup of coffee, nibbled at a biscuit. She'd

had nothing since yesterday lunch, but her throat was
parchment; even swallowing a major effort. Was this
what it felt like being Amy? Amy! She wondered if the
girl was enjoying her weekend, oblivious of the drama
she'd left behind her.

The telephone was a squat plastic machine on a table,
taunting her. It was so inhuman, yet it had such power
over lives! She hated it. Its silence rang out more
stridently than ever its bell could. This morning she
could hardly even bring herself to dial Karl's number
again—but she did. Nothing. She splashed her face with
water, changed into jeans and a warm jumper, turned
up the central heating which had been left on low for
the weekend. Slowly, deliberately, she walked downstairs to fetch her suitcase. It lay exactly where she'd left
it, of course—bulging with promise and equipment
suitable for a special trip to London. Feet dragging, she
carried it back upstairs and threw it on her bed.

By teatime she was in a kind of tragic trance. She
must, she had to eat something now—this was
ridiculous: foolish adolescents behaved this way, not
sensible young women. Without taste or appetite she
laboriously chewed her way through a honey sandwich
and drank a glass of milk. Three times more, she dialled
Elmhurst, but with less hope each time. Her finger
found its way automatically to the numbers by now,
independent of her numbed brain. No one was there.
She pictured it, heard the regular summons of the bell
reverberating through Karl's empty study from the
phone on his desk—next to the typewriter, the neat
piles of paper, the reference books. At last she covered
her face with her hands and wept uncontrollably.

Just after seven, exhausted and drained, she
undressed and crawled into bed. Her mind and body
had reached the end of their resources. She gave in to
them both and fell into a long restless sleep. She had
plenty of dreams, but forgot them all.

She was up early, dressed for a working day,
spooning the usual bowl of cereal into her unwilling

mouth. Purposefully she marched down to the shop, unpinned the notice that said she would be opening at two-thirty and turned the sign round to 'open'. Then she sat behind her desk, busy with Christmas lists. Life was going on. At an almost imperceptible level, her bleak fury with Nick was merging into a new resentment against Karl. So he'd had a severe shock and thought he'd been badly let down. That was no reason to vanish without trace—not to contact her, give her at least a chance to explain. It was all so simple and stupid; he had to believe her.

Somehow she got through a busy day, gritting her teeth and fixing a wooden smile for her customers' benefit. In the evening she remembered that Karl would be going over to Bodiam to pick up Amy. The weekend was officially at an end; the adventure that had never started.

She had never felt less hungry, but she knew her body needed fuel. She warmed a tin of soup, toasted two slices of wholemeal bread, managed to eat some of it. It was odd how misery tightened up one's insides, turned perfectly good food to dust in one's mouth. Then she sat and stared into the flickering television screen, seeing it but making no sense of it.

The sound of the doorbell seemed to echo in another world, as unreal and far-off as the film dancing meaninglessly in front of her eyes. With slow stiff movements she switched off the set, then went out into the hall and listened. It rang again—a forceful, imperious buzz. She shrugged, and moved down a few stairs towards it. Then she hesitated: suppose it was Nick? Or one of the family? Or a friend? This was no time to chat. It pealed once more, long and loud. Knowing it was neither Nick, nor a friend, she ran the rest of the way to the door, and opened it. Karl would be there, of course. Who else?

He was tall and magnetic, but dishevelled, weary. She had never seen him so weary—dark shadows around the sharp grey eyes, lines of stress running down from each corner of the long mouth. Scruffiest of denims, black hair unkempt. Even after long days and nights at the typewriter, he was never as wiped out as this.

Her heart had lurched and fluttered with hope at the sight of him, but it sank again when she studied his expression. It was not so much anger she read there, as a profound sadness. He wore his hurt on his face, and it tightened his lips to thin bands, hardened his eyes to steel. He was a wounded, disillusioned man who had struggled to accept the new emotional opportunities life seemed to be throwing in his path—and then stumbled up against treachery all over again.

'Are you alone?' His voice was clipped and cold.

'Who else would be here?' she heard herself, pushed on to the defensive, snapping back with a caustic retort.

His dry laugh grated, sandpaper to her ears. 'You tell *me*.'

She ran the tip of her tongue over parched lips. 'Karl, I . . . you'd better come in.' She stood aside to let him pass, then followed the dear, familiar form up the stairs. His step was deliberate but fast. He did not look back at her as he usually did, smiling down over his shoulder. She grew tense with foreboding.

'Coffee?' She hesitated in the living-room doorway.

'Nothing thanks.' He was already sitting down, legs stretched out and crossed at the ankles but body strangely stiff and formal, upright against the chair back. She sat in the armchair opposite, leaning forward, strained, alert. Anything they said now could shape their future. 'I haven't got much to say, Beth.' There was a dull mechanical quality in his tone which alarmed her, far more than violence. 'I've been doing a lot of thinking. I want to tell you what I've decided to do.'

The foreboding became pure dread. She was clammy all over, pale as death, but he hardly seemed to notice her. 'Karl, I know how you must feel—I know what you thought you saw—but you were wrong. You've got to let me tell you what was . . .' In her agitation her hands became fists, banging on the chair for emphasis.

But he shook his head, cutting in on her flow with stark, serrated words. 'I know what you're about to say. I don't want to hear it all again. We had that bit before—the wide-eyed innocence number—swearing Nick's been out of your system for three years, all that.' He closed his eyes and passed a hand across his brow, pushing back the tangled hair. 'I didn't come round here for an encore tonight. Save your breath.' The ghost of a wry grin hovered for an instant, and was gone. 'I'm the one that writes the plots—remember?'

This was impossible—even more gruesome than her worst fears. 'But Karl . . .'

'No, Beth. What can you say, except that it meant nothing? A tender scene like that *never* means nothing. I've had Nick's version and I can only too easily imagine yours. I wrote your script before I even got here,' he remarked bitterly.

Her stomach clenched as she fought a wave of nausea which threatened to engulf her. 'You've seen him, then.' Weakly she leaned back in her chair.

'Sure. He's back at the house now, with Amy. The poor kid doesn't know what hit her. She's wondering what the hell's going on.'

Beth winced with sheer pain to contemplate the child's bewilderment in the face of all this. 'I kept trying to 'phone you, but you weren't there.' If only, *if only* she'd got through to him in time to prevent Nick getting his malicious earful in first!

'I went off—I had to think. When I got back late Sunday night, Nick was skulking in a corner practising his invisible act.' His lips twisted scornfully. 'He's even more transparent than you, and I've got no more time to waste listening to his pathetic whinings. I was on the point of coming to see you then, but he insisted I stay and hear him out first. He seemed more confident than usual somehow, so I did. What he said stopped me in my tracks.' He brooded over at her.

Something in his tone injected ice into Beth's blood. She was having difficulty catching her breath. But she kept herself outwardly calm, folding her arms tightly across her chest as she leaned towards Karl. 'What did he say?'

He made a slight movement, hunching his shoulders. 'Oh, the predictable stuff about you and him seeing each other several times recently,' he announced evenly. 'How you've only been using Amy and me to keep a hold on him—how he's been busy fighting you off ever since you found out he was here and made a dead set at him. How you've always wanted him back, ever since . . .' He sighed, like a man expelling poisoned air from his lungs.

The black screen behind Beth's eyes was turning to vermilion as she took this in. 'And you're telling me you actually *accept* this . . .' she groped for scathing enough adjectives, 'sordid, ludicrous, petty tissue of lies?' Her voice rose up the scale, breathless with indignation. 'You know Nick would say anything to keep on the right side of you!'

'That's what I reckoned. I told him to get lost, and made for the door.' Karl's eyes narrowed, assessing her. 'Then he stopped me, said he had just one more thing to say and it might make some difference.'

She felt she might pass out—but that was no mature escape route. 'What?'

'You don't know?'

'I can't imagine,' she asserted truthfully. She had nothing to hide—had she?

'Dear little brother-in-law pointed out that you were not the first young lady to latch on to me. Intellectual gold-diggers, he calls them. Literary groupies is another choice description I've heard used,' he sneered. 'Oh, I've had a few—out for what they can get, or just picking up thrills, an aura of reflected glamour from a big name.' His eyes followed her reaction very closely. 'After all, Nick said, books are your world. What would suit you better than a nice juicy writer to get your teeth into— even better than a nice juicy book?' He paused, head on one side, observing her quizzically. 'I commented that as far as that idea goes, you didn't even know who I was. To you I'm just Karl Franklyn—an unknown minor scribbler. Any attachment you have to me—and Amy—is purely personal. That's what makes it so special,' he added, suddenly intense.

'And what did he say to that?' Her voice and gaze dropped, defeated. She knew the answer only too well; and cursed herself for letting Nick nose out this one small harmless deception and then play it against her— a trump card, an ace.

'He swore you've known who I am all the time. He said I should ask you myself.' His eyes exerted a physical pull, forcing hers to meet them. 'So, I'm asking you. Do you know who I am, Beth?'

Denial would be pointless; it was always useless, compounding one falsehood with another. And was it so bad, anyway, to have hugged this warm secret to herself? She met his challenge boldly. 'Yes Karl, I do. I've known you were Frank Charles since the first day. I was going to tell you, this weekend.' Her voice cracked as she turned sharply away.

'How? How did you find out? Did Nick tell you?' He was fierce, accusing.

'I guessed,' she told him simply.

'Guessed? How?' Acute scepticism vibrated from every cell of him.

'From your name—and I saw your picture in one of your books. It was Amy who dropped the first hint, asking me if I liked your work. She didn't tell me who you were, though,' she interjected, anxious not to implicate Amy in his general wrath. It was bad enough having him furious with her, without involving the girl.

'And do you?' he queried keenly. 'Like my work?'

'I do. Very much. I always have—for years, since I first discovered it. But that's got nothing at all to do with why I like you—or Amy.' These last words emerged almost on a whisper; and of course they were only partly true. Her love for his art was bound up with her love for him—but not in the way he meant. How could she expect a man so obsessively private, guarded, to understand that?

He spread his fingers in a gesture of dejected resignation. 'My case rests.'

'You mean—because I didn't come clean about that straight away, you won't take my word on anything else?' Q.E.D. She was aghast at the inhuman logic.

'Try to see it my way. I was already upset. Nick told me that—so cocky, so sure—and it was like a door slamming inside my head. A light went out. I lost all grip on myself. I thought I was finding out how to trust again . . . feelings . . . all snuffed out like a candle when I heard . . .' He stood now and paced the room, hands thrust deep into pockets, emanating the grim despair of a trapped creature. 'I've had as much as I can take of being used—pushed around. I thought you really were different, Beth.' It was a shout of agony—hoarse, moving.

'I am.' She could only mutter the assurance, suddenly hopeless and helpless.

'Maybe. But now I don't know what to think. I have to put space between us, you and me, Beth.' He stopped short a few feet from her, confronting her. 'I'm taking Amy back to Vancouver.'

'NO!' It was a blunt instrument, battering her skull. 'You can't!'

'I can, and I'm going to.' Reaching the crunch, he became firm and level. 'As soon as possible. We can have the rest of our stuff sent on. I need time to find out what's really going on inside me—think the thing through. Maybe get some real writing done. I've been too—distracted to concentrate, here.' Was she even to blame for that? she wondered desolately. 'Who knows?' he piled it on deep. 'Caroline might even have decided to go back. Nick as good as admitted he has no idea where she went.' Every word was barbed, a nail in Beth's coffin; but she was far too frozen to move, or even speak. 'Try to understand, Beth. I might be in touch sometime—if not—well, it was good while it lasted, hey?' The absurd, meaningless cliché taunted the air between them.

Not again! her tormented mind was screeching; but only stiffly cool phrases could force a way out. 'What about Amy?'

He was immovable, hard. 'Amy ought to be at school. She's one hell of a lot better—oh yes, I know,' he acknowledged, catching the wry lift of her eyebrows, 'largely thanks to your expert ministrations.' Expert? There was nothing expert about them. They were based on sheer affection, instinctive feeling. 'But you knew we had to go back home eventually, Beth. You knew.'

Where was the point in hurling herself against the dense wall he'd erected around his emotions—armour against all dangerous contact, perhaps forever? So, this was how it had to finish: *not with a bang but with a whimper*, as a poet once said. All those glorious newborn hopes and passions, pulverised to a mere pulp of memories—fodder for fantasies and useless dreams in the endless empty nights ahead.

And then there would be books. His books, other books—the safe cardboard world she knew so well, where no one let you down, least of all yourself. It appeared that after all the future looked much the same as the past—dreary, shapeless. 'Goodbye then, Karl.' No more to be said. She might as well bow out with some dignity intact. 'Tell Amy if she wants to write . . .' she rescued the tremor that invaded the cold, unreal words, 'she knows where I am.' *And so do you*, her heart cried out to him in anguish.

Surprisingly, he held out a hand. 'I'm sorry it has to end this way. I guess I'm not ready for . . . I guess I'll never be ready again.' His eyes and voice were harsh with pain suffered and inflicted.

Surely not a twinge of regret, after so much recrimination? If he was the uncertain one now, she was brittle, merciless. 'Don't drag it out, Karl. You've done what you came to do. Nothing I say will change it. Now go away and leave me to get on with my life in peace.'

'Beth.' His eyes drilled into hers, searching, questing. For God's sake, did he expect her to go down on her knees and implore him to stay?

Bitterness surged in her as she drew the bottom line at last. 'Get out!' She bit the order off between clenched teeth, explosive. 'Just get out of here!'

He got out—swung round, left the room, left the house. Left her sitting in her chair, staring straight ahead, as hard and still as stone.

It was a fortnight to Christmas. Beth plunged herself into frenzied activity—numbed, dazed, sealed off from reality by a layer of what felt like solid concrete. Her mind and body told her she was in severe shock. Her heart went into limbo and produced no feedback at all, not even at night, when she expected to lie and suffer but only lay and merged with the enveloping blackness. She seemed to have no edge, no definition at all. She was surprised people could even see her. She just went on, being but not being; living, but scarcely alive.

She made no further attempt to contact them, and within a few days she assumed they'd left. Bleakness settled on her soul like a vast vulture, poised to pounce the moment she was foolish enough to let a feeling through. Her one aim in life was to keep it at bay. Being so busy in the shop helped in a way, but underneath she knew it was only putting off the evil hour.

The evil hour was bound to come—she knew because she'd been through it before, only this time it was far, far worse. Exactly a week after Karl's last visit she woke up in the morning and the concrete had dissolved overnight. The raw fact of her situation hit home at last in the form of a massive, monstrous depression. She could just about move as far as the 'phone to warn her mother that she wasn't too well and planned to shut the shop and come over. Christmas was only a week away; she'd have closed two days before in any case. The bulk of the seasonal trade was done. She could afford to let go—even if she'd had any choice.

Within the hour Sally was at the door, letting herself in with the family's spare key, bustling round Beth who still lay in bed—pale, listless and weak. She'd kept on her feet, but she'd had virtually no appetite, and it showed.

'What on earth have you been doing with yourself, Bethy?' Sally was all cheery concern as she sat Beth up and watched sternly over her while she drank tea and tackled a boiled egg without enthusiasm. 'You look a real wreck.'

'Thanks a lot.' Beth dunked a strip of bread and butter valiantly into her yolk. Sally had taken one look at her older sister's drawn face and recognised a desperate need for reassurance. When they were children, boiled eggs with 'soldiers' had been one of their favourites. Beth managed a wan smile as she accepted the younger girl's affectionate gesture.

Sally peered into her face. 'Beth, why didn't you tell us you were feeling bad? Has something happened?' She sat on the bed beside her.

'I didn't tell you because I was feeling quite okay,' Beth told her mildly. 'And yes, something has happened, but I don't want to go into it now.'

With more tact and wisdom than usual, Sally did not push the point. She simply helped Beth to dress and pack a few things (including a carefully-prepared bag of presents for them all) and see that everything was in a fit state to leave—in the shop as well as the flat. Then she carried Beth's holdall out to the car while Beth walked—slowly, stiffly as if in a dream—beside her.

'Like me to drive?' Sally offered as Beth fumbled with her keys, all thumbs.

'Yes please, Sal.' Beth handed the bunch of keys gratefully to her sister. As she climbed into the car, a thought struck her. 'How did you get here?'

'Drew brought me. He had to come over anyway,' Sally explained glibly.

Beth knew quite well he hadn't had to at all, but there was a glimmer of comfort in the knowledge that they were rallying quietly round her.

For five days she haunted the fringes of family life, helping as best she could with festive preparations, trying not to be the spectre at the feast. She did at least stay upright, but several times a day she found it necessary to escape to the bedroom she shared with Sally so that she could shed a few tears in private, or just sit and come to terms with her pain. She was the first to condemn self-pity, but she understood the difference between that and facing grief out. If you didn't let yourself mourn a deep loss it stayed with you the rest of your life, sapping your strength.

Her family understood it too, and never swamped her, merely continuing to offer easygoing support when she needed it. They refrained from asking direct questions about her problem, but they could hardly help throwing curious glances in her direction and speculating behind her back. All families, even the kindest ones, do that. She never mentioned the Franklyns, and that in itself was enough to tell them the reason for her distress. With a discretion that was almost funny, they all kept off the subject as religiously as she did. Just once, in an unguarded moment, her mother made a passing remark to her about Amy—and Beth's involuntary wince and flush spoke volumes, making Val bite her lip and wish she'd kept her thoughts to herself.

Christmas Eve was always frenetic on the farm. Every possible chore had to be got out of the way so that there was a minimum to do on the day itself. Lynne and Sally helped Joe and Drew with the stock and outdoor jobs while Val, Beth and Paul busied themselves with last-minute preparing and cooking.

Beth felt as calm and contained as she'd managed all week. Sometimes her suffering was a sensation of part of her wrenched away, leaving a bleeding wound which refused to scar. Today it was more like a tight knot, a clamp deep inside her. While she was here, buffered by attention and affection, thrown back into a childlike irresponsibility, she might survive; but how could she face the prospect of reopening the shop in the lonely chill days of the new year?

Amy and Karl had been gone two weeks. In one way it seemed a lifetime. At another, more real level, her mind refused to believe they'd gone at all. They were so vivid, so vital. How could they be so many miles away? Somewhere she'd never been, never seen? How were they? Was Amy very unhappy, or was she still getting better? Did she miss Beth as much as Beth missed her?

And then there was Karl . . . she tried to avoid even forming his name in her head, but it grew there of its own accord, all the time. His absence, the way he'd left, was a physical ache, and it gripped her body and racked her spirit, intensifying rather than easing with each day. She knew in her heart that no one else could ever fill that gap he'd created in her life. She might accept the loss of him, eventually—but she'd never really get over it.

As she stood on a stool, adjusting the star at the top of the fine Christmas tree in the lounge, someone shouted for her from the kitchen. It sounded important so she jumped down and followed the sound—to find Lynne, in muddy wellingtons, red-faced and panting, waiting for her in the back doorway.

'I can't come in,' she explained breathlessly, indicating her boots, 'but there's a message for you.' Her normally placid face was strangely alight.

'A message?' Puzzled, Beth tried to read her sister's expression.

'You've got to go to the front yard. Dad's got something to show you. Now.'

'Dad?' Beth frowned; but Lynne was off and away back to the cows, clumping in her heavy boots, grinning as she ran.

Wondering what her father was playing at, Beth hurried back through the house, grabbing her jacket in the hall, and emerged from the front door, looking about for Joe. It was cold and damp and nearly dusk; she wrapped her arms around herself as she stood on the doorstep, her breath rising on the chill misty air.

There was no sign of Joe, or of anyone, as far as she could see. Shrugging, she turned to go in—then stopped dead, gasping, her hand flying to cover her mouth. Parked unobtrusively in the line of cars, between Andrew's old van and Joe's Landrover, was a big green Saab. It might have been there all the time, it fitted so neatly; but Beth knew full well it hadn't. Fixed to the spot, she stared over at it—her eyes wide with astonishment but her legs immobilised.

As soon as its two occupants saw her looking their way they tumbled out—doors slamming, footsteps crunching on the gravel of the drive. Then they were shouting and running to meet her—the tall dark man and the slender blonde girl—and Beth's legs sprang into action to sweep her towards them. The three of them met in the middle of the yard to merge into a mutual, triple hug and huddle.

'Beth—oh, Beth!' Amy laughed and cried at the same time. 'I've missed you so much—oh, Beth!'

The Porters appeared from all sides as if on a secret summons, to add their greetings and cries of welcome, showing only a bare touch of surprise. Soon Amy found herself borne off with Paul and Sally to admire the decorations. After a few minutes everyone seemed to melt away, leaving Karl and Beth standing alone in a twilit, mysterious winter world.

Not touching, they stared into one another's faces for long moments. Karl's eyes were deep, brimming with wordless messages, lingering on her every feature as if to assure themselves everything was as he recalled it. Delight gave way to concern, then remorse as he registered the change in her.

'Oh, my poor lady. My dearest woman.' The beloved voice, dark and husky with contained emotion, flowed over her, healing. He reached out to take her in his arms, and she went to him naturally, joyfully, without hesitation. 'You're so tired and unhappy. What the hell have I put you through? Oh God—Beth!'

She buried herself in the wonderful warmth of him, breathing the well-remembered scents of him through the thick sweater. A thousand questions reared up and she pushed them aside, content now to feel his powerful presence so close again. 'Never mind,' she whispered, the joyful truth of it only just penetrating through. 'You've come back. You're back, Karl.'

Her words were all but lost against his chest, but he leaned down to catch them. 'I'm back. I'm back—and I should never have left. I'm a damn fool, Beth.' His cheek nuzzled the top of her head, and he groaned and tightened his hold on her. 'It was like a—a demon taking me over, my darling ... I had to leave you before I knew ... I had to go, so that I could come back. Can you ever understand?'

She understood everything at that moment, and none of it mattered. Pulling away, she lifted a radiant face to his, studying him now with loving care. He was as tense and strained as she was, but the terrifying dulled, shuttered grimness had fallen clean away. 'Come on.' Holding out her hand to him, she moved towards the house. 'It's cold here.' Catching up, he took it, automatically linking his fingers with hers. They walked in step through the hall, up the stairs to her room. All around them, muffled behind various doors, echoed laughter and conversation, seasonal excitement. But no one came to interfere with them.

She shut the door and pulled him down beside her on the bed. Wonderingly she reached up to touch his face—the skin shadowed and roughened with a day's growth of beard—running a finger along the sensitive line of his lips. He was really there. He existed. And he'd come back.

He might have read her thoughts through her glowing eyes. Smiling, he took her face in his hands to gaze down into it. In a single, gentle, subtle, familiar movement, he took her glasses from her nose and set them carefully

on the bedside cabinet. Then his hands were on her
shoulders, drawing her to him, his mouth seeking,
claiming hers at last. The universal, eternal language
bonded them—expressed what words never can say—
and Beth knew it would always be with them.

When the hunger swelled up, threatening to
overwhelm them, Karl drew reluctantly, tantalisingly
away. This was the time to hold her very close, his
strong arms firmly around her, his steady heartbeat in
unison with hers. There would be other times—many
times, over many years—to satisfy the craving. And as
often as it was satisfied, it would never be fulfilled. That
was the wonder of it.

From downstairs, domestic noises floated up to them,
reminders of a world they belonged to, yet were
separated from. Beth nestled dreamily against a
shoulder she'd never thought to lean on again. 'Is Amy
all right, Karl?' She had to know.

'She will be, now.' She felt the rough edge of his self-
reproach. 'Poor kid, she's had a terrible fortnight. I can
hardly bear to tell you, Beth. As soon as we got back I
knew I'd made the biggest mistake of my life. Even
before we left, Amy seemed to shrivel in front of my
eyes. She wouldn't eat a thing. She pined and moped.
All she'd talk about was you, and everything here. I was
a crazy, crass idiot, plucking her out of—all she was
finding here; thinking it was okay to just dump her
down in the old environment. There's nothing for her
there. She hated me, and I don't blame her. Despair
made me selfish. I don't know what got into me. I can
only ask you both to forgive me.'

At the end of this long, agonised speech he seemed to
crumple against her. She knelt on the bed, taking his
hands, staring deep into his suffering eyes. 'Of course
we will. And you do know what got into you, Karl. It
was sheer blind panic. You've been too hurt, you didn't
want to be hurt any more. How could you be sure of
me—after what you saw and what you found out? How
could you be?'

'You're so right.' With a low, fierce sound, somewhere between a sigh and a moan, he clasped her against him. 'You're so wise. Wise, and good, and lovely. You're the most beautiful woman I've ever known, and I love you.'

Such a rush of sweetness sang through her, she thought she'd faint with joy. He'd once talked of miracles. This was the miracle. 'And I love you, Karl.'

He kissed her again then, long and deep, and when he released her he smiled down into dazed brown eyes. It was the tenderest smile she'd ever seen. 'Shall I tell you,' he offered, 'what Amy decided on the plane over today?'

Beth returned the smile. 'Go on.'

'She's got it all settled. You're going to marry me, and we're going to buy Elmhurst and make it into a palace, and live there happily ever after. You have to keep the shop, because Amy likes it, and I have to write lots of even more brilliant best-sellers with you beside me. And we have to have two, maybe three, perfect kids for Amy to help with—when she can spare the time, that is.'

'Oh, Karl.' Despite her wistful grin at this idealised, adolescent scenario, a shadow crossed Beth's face. 'Dear Amy. If it was only that simple.'

'Couldn't it be that simple?' He was serious now. 'I told you, Beth, I've got nothing to go back there for. It's the scene of too much heartbreak. I had to find out the hard way—for us all.' His brow creased wearily. 'But at least I know for sure now. Amy says home is where the heart is. So, our home must be right here, with you. Wherever you are. I love Elmhurst.' He was warming up now to his persuasive theme. 'I know you liked it. I know I can work there—as long as you're with me.'

'But . . .' Her gaze left his, dropping to her hands. Hadn't he forgotten one major obstacle? 'What about—about Caroline?' she muttered.

He clutched his head. 'I'm a fool—I don't know where I am—jet-lag, seeing you again, I don't know . . . I haven't told you the half of it yet. I just wanted to hear you say yes. I feel as if I've never been away from you. I expect you to know it all, by telepathy.' He grinned ruefully.

'Know what?' She followed his moods and expressions, knowing, loving each one.

'When I got back there was a letter from Caroline waiting with my lawyers. I called them, and they told me. She wants a divorce. She wants to marry this actor guy, in California. I could hardly believe it when I heard. She actually wants to settle down again, Beth! For now, at least.' His mouth twitched wryly. 'I'm free. Free, Beth. After a few months, I can marry you.'

'Free?' She studied him dubiously. There were ways and ways of being free.

'Sure.' Reading her uncertain expression, he lifted a surprised eyebrow. 'Beth, you surely can't think . . .? I haven't wanted Caroline for years. I kept on trying so long just for Amy's sake. The kid seemed so desperate. What else could I do? She loved her mother—or so I thought. *She* did; *I* didn't.'

'No, I wasn't sure about that,' she confessed carefully, hardly daring to trust what she was hearing. 'And what about Amy? When she heard the news? Did she . . .'

'She didn't turn a hair. I could hardly believe it. I was amazed. She just said: "Great, now you'll be able to marry Beth." The last thing she seemed to want was to see her mother again. After all, Caroline never showed more than a passing interest in her.' He paused, playing back the film of grim memories; perhaps savouring the finality of it at last. 'All she could do was talk about you, my Beth. I told you,' he touched her cheek almost reverently, 'you're miraculous.'

In its way, that was the most wonderful revelation of all. 'I'm so glad, Karl.'

'So, lady—what about this next chapter she's written for us?' he urged.

But Beth wasn't ready yet to accept her destiny. There were still ends to be tied up, unknown quantities to be brought to light. 'What about Nick?'

'Oh, I stopped worrying about him as soon as I realised I couldn't make it without you. Whatever he was doing there that day, I know you'll tell me about it in your own sweet time. I trust you, Beth. I should have trusted you all along.'

'Where is he now?'

'I kicked him out at last—before we even flew back,' he informed her, with clear satisfaction. 'He left the same day. I guess he knew when he was finally licked. Last thing I gave him was the other half of his return ticket—I think he went to the States. If he ever shows his face to us again, or makes any more trouble, he'll get more than he's ever bargained for.' He grinned crookedly. 'I don't know how I've kept my hands off him all these years.' An old tension curled his hands into tight fists. It had taken more willpower to control his hatred and resentment against Nick, first for Caroline's sake, then Amy's, than any outsider could have guessed.

'Somehow, I don't think he'll make any trouble,' Beth reflected. 'I should imagine he's had enough of us all by now. I expect he'll go and find his sister.'

'Now then, Miss Porter.' Karl beetled with mock impatience. 'Any more flimsy excuses, or are you going to give me my answer?'

'One more, Mr Charles. Have you forgiven me for not confessing to my inside knowledge of your true identity?' she enquired solemnly.

'Oh, that.' Sighing, he pulled her to him, stroking her hair back from her forehead. 'I was a confounded idiot about that too. Why shouldn't you pick it up, with your quick eye and mind? Amy was kind of tough on me when I told her about that. She pointed out that it was just like you, not to let on you knew, because you'd guess I wouldn't like people to know. She really put me in my place. I felt about an inch tall.' He pouted, comically chastened.

Beth laughed happily. 'She was dead right, of course. I was all set to tell you, that weekend. I love your books, Karl. I've admired them since long before I met you, or ever expected to meet you. It only made it more exciting when I knew who you were. But it's you I fell in love with—not Frank Charles.'

'I know it now. And I'm deeply honoured by your admiration. I shall endeavour to continue to earn it.' He bowed satirically. 'And since you mention that weekend that never was . . .' he grimaced, 'allow me to invite my most valued critic to spend many, many weekends in London with me. I intend, quite blatantly, to sleep my way to the top of her good opinion. She and I have plenty of catching up to do.'

His voice sank from light-hearted banter to a low, fierce intensity. His hands seized her shoulders again, his lips were hard and demanding on hers. At last, breathing heavily, he tore himself away. 'I love you, Beth—and I need you. Take me on—take the risk—marry me, stay with me, please.'

She took his head between gentle hands and pulled it down to cover his face with butterfly kisses. Her heart would surely burst with the love she had for him. 'I'll take you on, Karl—and Amy—and Elmhurst—and as much of the rest of her fantasy as we can manage to produce,' she promised—vibrant with certainty.

'Beth; Beth—I don't deserve you, but I'll do anything I can to make you happy.' It was an overflow of emotion, muttered against her mouth.

'Just be there.' For a last, long instant they clung together. Then she jumped up, holding out both hands to him. 'Now, I think we've lurked up here long enough. My family's a tolerant lot, but they'll want to share our news too.'

He took her hands and came to his feet beside her. 'Unless young Amy's thought fit to inform them already. She had more confidence in my powers of persuasion than I did,' he remembered, with self-deprecating irony.

Downstairs, cosy among holly and tinsel and glittering lights, the others were assembled over tea. Amy sat next to Paul, sedate and contained—and not far from a picture adorned with a large sprig of mistletoe. Her cheeks were delicately flushed, her blue eyes sparkled—and she was tucking into a generous slice of cake with every sign of enjoyment.

She beamed over at her father and Beth as they entered, hand in hand, and stood pressed close together near the door. 'Val says we can spend Christmas here, Dad. Isn't that great?'

'Great.' Karl smiled at Val and Joe, who smiled warmly back. 'Thanks,' he said.

'Why didn't you *tell* us?' grumbled Paul accusingly. 'We didn't get you any presents!'

'Who needs presents?' Amy glanced luminously at him. 'It's just good to be here, that's all.' Everyone grinned back at her, lit up in her glow—except Sally, who was staring wistfully at Karl and Beth in their pool of fluorescent happiness. 'Oh, and by the way Dad,' Amy announced airily, 'I'm going to school with Paul and Lynne. Paul says it's a real nice school. If we come to live here properly, it'll be my nearest school too so I'll have to go there. I'll be in fourth grade,' she explained grandly. 'Paul's in fifth,' she added proudly.

Karl looked from his radiant daughter to his newly-adopted extended family. 'Well, that seems to be all fixed up then,' he assented gravely. 'We'll have to get busy with our applications.'

'Oh, and I've told them our other news,' Amy went on nonchalantly. She flashed a broad grin at Beth; then a crack of anxiety showed through. 'He has asked you, hasn't he?'

Beth's warm dark eyes shone back, and her grasp tightened on Karl's hand as she smiled up at him, then round at her parents, her brothers and sisters—a collection of eager, loving faces, all turned enquiringly in her direction. One day she'd have a whole lot more to tell them all; but this would do for a start.

'Yes, he's asked me, Amy,' she replied serenely. 'And since you've already spread the good word, it's just as well I've accepted, isn't it?'

Harlequin Romance

Coming Next Month

2761 STRANGER IN TOWN Kerry Allyne
An Australian storekeeper is convinced all gold prospectors are daydreamers, living in a fantasy. Then, falling in love with one of them brings a change of mind—and heart!

2762 THE DRIFTWOOD DRAGON Ann Charlton
Haunted by his past, an Australian film star is overjoyed when he finds a woman whose love helps him to shed his typecast image—until his brother's interference almost ruins their chance for happiness.

2763 VOWS OF THE HEART Susan Fox
Returning for physical and emotional recovery to the Wyoming ranch where she'd always felt secure, an interior designer discovers her adolescent crush for its owner has turned to love.

2764 AMARYLLIS DREAMING Samantha Harvey
Katy finds a man on Amaryllis Island, but not the father she seeks. She finally has to admit, though, that this powerful island overlord is destined to make all her dreams come true.

2765 ASK ME NO QUESTIONS Valerie Parv
Trusting her adventurer husband once lead to heartbreak for a Brisbane art-gallery owner. Her return, years later, when she's thinking of marrying someone else, faces her with a once-in-a-lifetime choice.

2766 TO BRING YOU JOY Essie Summers
A living legacy gives a young New Zealander the chance to prove her descent from the historic Beauchamps. But her benefactor, dear Aunt Amabel, wants her niece to find adventure—and love.

Available in May wherever paperback books are sold, or through Harlequin Reader Service.

In the U.S.
P.O. Box 1397
Buffalo, N.Y.
14240-1397

In Canada
P.O. Box 2800, Postal Sation A
5170 Yonge Street
Willowdale, Ontario M2N 6J3

What readers say about Harlequin romance fiction...

"I absolutely adore Harlequin romances! They are fun and relaxing to read, and each book provides a wonderful escape."
—N.E.,* Pacific Palisades, California

"Harlequin is the best in romantic reading."
—K.G.,* Philadelphia, Pennsylvania

"Harlequins have been my passport to the world. I have been many places without ever leaving my doorstep."
—P.Z.,* Belvedere, Illinois

"My praise for the warmth and adventure your books bring into my life."
—D.F.,* Hicksville, New York

"A pleasant way to relax after a busy day."
—P.W.,* Rector, Arkansas

*Names available on request.

Can you keep a secret?

You can keep this one plus 4 free novels

Take 4 novels and a surprise gift FREE

Six exciting series for you every month... from Harlequin

Harlequin Romance·
The series that started it all

Tender, captivating and heartwarming...
love stories that sweep you off to faraway places
and delight you with the magic of love.

◆

Harlequin Presents·
Powerful contemporary love stories...as individual as the women who read them

The No. 1 romance series...
exciting love stories for you, the woman of today...
a rare blend of passion and dramatic realism.

◆

Harlequin Superromance®
It's more than romance...
it's Harlequin Superromance

A sophisticated, contemporary romance-fiction
series, providing you with a longer,
more involving read...a richer mix of complex plots,
realism and adventure.

WORLDWIDE LIBRARY IS YOUR TICKET TO ROMANCE, ADVENTURE AND EXCITEMENT

Experience it all in these big, bold Bestsellers— Yours exclusively from WORLDWIDE LIBRARY WHILE QUANTITIES LAST

To receive these Bestsellers, complete the order form, detach and send together with your check or money order (include 75¢ postage and handling), payable to WORLDWIDE LIBRARY, to:

In the U.S.
WORLDWIDE LIBRARY
901 Fuhrmann Blvd.
Buffalo, N.Y. 14269

In Canada
WORLDWIDE LIBRARY
P.O. Box 2800, 5170 Yonge Street
Postal Station A, Willowdale, Ontario
M2N 6J3

- -

Quant.	Title	Price
_____	**WILD CONCERTO**, Anne Mather	$2.95
_____	**A VIOLATION**, Charlotte Lamb	$3.50
_____	**SECRETS**, Sheila Holland	$3.50
_____	**SWEET MEMORIES**, LaVyrle Spencer	$3.50
_____	**FLORA**, Anne Weale	$3.50
_____	**SUMMER'S AWAKENING**, Anne Weale	$3.50
_____	**FINGER PRINTS**, Barbara Delinsky	$3.50
	DREAMWEAVER,	
_____	Felicia Gallant/Rebecca Flanders	$3.50
_____	**EYE OF THE STORM**, Maura Seger	$3.50
_____	**HIDDEN IN THE FLAME**, Anne Mather	$3.50
_____	**ECHO OF THUNDER**, Maura Seger	$3.95
_____	**DREAM OF DARKNESS**, Jocelyn Haley	$3.95

	YOUR ORDER TOTAL	$_____
	New York and Arizona residents add appropriate sales tax	$_____
	Postage and Handling	$___.75
	I enclose	$_____

NAME _____

ADDRESS _____ APT.# _____

CITY _____

STATE/PROV. _____ ZIP/POSTAL CODE _____
WW-1-3